THE DARK AWAKENING

THE CHOSEN COVEN
BOOK ONE

D. L. BLADE

Social Media :
Instagram : booksbydlblade
Facebook : dlblade
Twitter : DLBlade_Writer

Editing by Christina Kaye www.xtinakayebooks.com
Formatted by Affordable formatting
All photographs by photographer Scott James Photography
Book design by Redbird Designs

Printed and bound in the United States of America.
First printing edition October 2018.

Independently Published by D.L. Blade
http://www.dlbladebooks.com

This book is dedicated to the strongest person I know:
My mother.

CHAPTER ONE

They were there in the shadows again. This was the third time this week I had thought I was being watched. The first time, I was getting out of my car to walk into the house when I heard the rustling of leaves and the crackling sound of old fallen branches beneath someone's feet. I quickly turned on the flashlight from my phone, but when the light pierced the darkness, the sound stopped.

Tonight, it was a silhouette behind my aunt Lily's fence in the backyard. It wasn't someone walking by with their dog, or a neighbor taking out their trash. They were standing there, watching me as I walked to the sink to rinse my dinner bowl. I wasn't going to tell her again. She'd just tell me what she told me the last time I brought it up. She'd say I was just seeing things and that it was normal to feel this way after trauma.

"Your turn, Mercy," Lily said, pulling my gaze from the window.

"All right, all right. I'm coming. Are you that eager to lose?" I teased.

I took one last glance out the window. They were gone.

Maybe I am imagining things.

My two best girlfriends just rolled their eyes at me, and my ex-boyfriend, Riley, sat there patiently. He smiled in my direction as I sat down.

Lily tucked her short brown strands behind her left ear and

looked down at her glass. She took a sip of her red wine, gripping her glass firmly, while her index finger tapped gently and rhythmically on the side of the slender wine glass.

I looked over at Cami and Shannon, who were watching Lily as she set the wine glass down on the table, shaking her head as she giggled softly.

I met my two girlfriends, Cami and Shannon, at cheerleading camp the summer before our freshmen year in high school. Shannon had beautiful, dark olive skin, raven-black hair, and stunning blue eyes. Cami proudly wore her signature ponytail tight against the back of her head, keeping her long blonde locks from falling in her face. Her thinly plucked eyebrows were shaped into the perfect arch, which complemented the curves of her eyes.

On a typical Friday night, the two of them would be dolled up and ready for a night out, makeup done and dressed to impress, but it was a Wednesday game night in, so the two of them were wearing sweatpants, tank tops, and little to no makeup. For me, on the other hand, that was my normal attire. I hated dressing up. I was happy in my yoga pants or ripped jeans and T-shirts that often consisted of my favorite band logos. I didn't look like a tomboy or anything. I still styled my long, dark brown, wavy hair and slapped on some mascara to complement my bright emerald cat-shaped eyes.

"You're going to draw this one out, aren't you?" Lily asked, trying to hide her yawn by covering her wide-open mouth with her hand. "Not too long, though. It's getting late."

Even though my mind had been distracted by what I thought I had seen outside, I pulled my focus back onto the game we had been playing, Battle-Star Frontier. A brief glance at the clock told me we had been playing the game for over three hours. My head was fogging over, and my lower back ached from sitting on acrylic chairs for so long. I stretched out my legs, took a deep breath, and gave my cards a once-over. I just needed to roll an eight.

Cami lowered her brow and huffed. "I can't keep my eyes open anymore." She grabbed her water, took a swig, and glanced down at her phone, probably checking the time.

"I'll drive your car. My energy drink is doing its job keeping me alive right now," Shannon joked.

Riley flashed me his handsome grin again and shook his head. I glanced around the table one last time and gently tossed the two dice, so they didn't roll off the table. One die landed right in front of me, showing five red dots, and the other landed in front of Riley.

"It's a three." Riley beamed.

An eight!

"Dang it!" Shannon tossed the remaining cards onto the table. "Surprise, surprise. Mercy wins again."

I applauded myself and moved my hips from side to side in a victory dance while I grabbed the last Battle-Star, which would gain me the final, winning point.

Once I placed my Battle-Star down on the table, Riley grabbed my knee and my leg jerked to the side at his touch.

I looked up at his boyish face. He formed a small crease with his brow as he cursed under his breath. Thankfully, everyone else was so preoccupied with cleaning up their game pieces, no one had noticed.

I leaned in toward Riley. "We need to talk."

"I didn't mean—"

"I know," I said sharply. "We still need to talk."

"Sorry." His voice cracked and he lowered his head. This absolutely killed me. Riley was the nicest guy I had ever known, and I was crushing his spirit.

What is wrong with me?

Shannon looked over at us. "Sorry for what?"

"Nothing," I quickly responded on his behalf. He stood up from the table and calmly walked out the backdoor. I hesitated, deciding not to follow him.

I'll give him a minute.

Cami looked around the room at everyone. "What's with him?"

Lily, too, had been watching the awkward encounter, and quickly stood up. "Do you girls care for anything else to eat?" She placed the lid on the game box and gestured toward the pot of homemade chili she had cooked for us.

Lily was an amazing cook and no matter how tired or stressed she was, made sure everyone visiting her home had a home-cooked meal ready for them. She'd never had kids of her own but taking care of me as if she were my own mother was natural for her. She looked to Cami for a response.

"We're good, Lily. Thank you," Cami responded for the both of them as she handed Shannon her keys.

She gripped the keys and turned to face me while pulling her purse over her shoulder. "Are you joining us tomorrow?"

"Yeah. Just not too early. I want to sleep in." I sounded whinier than I meant to. Shannon always scheduled our Thursday morning breakfast meetups for eight in the morning since we had graduated.

"I really need to go, guys. I have to put my mom to bed," Cami said as she tapped her foot impatiently.

Cami's mom, Laurie, was an alcoholic. I honestly couldn't recall if I had ever seen her without a bottle of booze in her hand, often drinking herself into a senseless stupor. Consequently, Cami found herself taking on the maternal role. On way too many nights, she put her drunken mother to sleep, usually helping to clean her of her own mess.

We felt so bad for Cami. No teenager should be wasting their youth by parenting their parent. Not to mention the danger she placed her daughter in every time she got so drunk.

Cami would be heading off to Parson's School of Design in New York soon. It would be the perfect escape, so she didn't have to be in that house anymore. We all were thankful for that, but we weren't sure what was going to happen to Laurie. We often talked about how we hoped she would willingly choose to go to rehab, but it was a long shot. She repeatedly told her daughter that she didn't have a problem.

"Where do you guys want to meet?" I asked.

"Probably Tippy's Pancake House. It just opened last weekend," Cami answered.

I looked at her curiously. "Tippy as in Ryan 'Tippy' Harrison?"

"The one and only."

Ryan was in his mid-forties. He had moved here with his grandmother Joanne about a year ago from Los Angeles, after his parents had become too old to take care of her. Los Angeles was just a little too loud and chaotic for his grandma, so they had decided to move to a smaller, quieter town. Ryan hadn't worked since he had arrived here. He was living off royalties from a few songs he had written while living the Hollywood dream. He did tell us once he was going to start a business out here, but he wasn't sure what his heart was leading him to do. I guess he figured it out—pancakes.

"Well, good for him. And, yes, that works," I said.

Shannon glanced over toward the window facing the backyard where Riley was waiting for me. "Call me if you need me." Shannon offered me an empty wish of good luck with a strained smile and a shrug, as if to express how uncomfortable she knew the moment would be for Riley and me.

"I'll fill you in at breakfast. Riley has a job working on Miss Darla's car, so he won't be there."

Cami moved past Shannon to give me a warm hug, but I tensed. I always hid my discomfort when someone touched me. Someday I hoped I'd get better, but in this moment, I wasn't ready. After Cami released me, Shannon followed her lead, and came in for a hug. I took a deep breath in and counted to five in my head. As I was slowly letting out my breath, she released me from the suffocating embrace.

As they walked toward Cami's car, I sent them off with a wave. Closing the door behind them, I secured the bottom lock and strolled into the kitchen to see if Lily needed help cleaning up. I knew she'd tell me not to bother, but I always offered anyway.

Lily's 1950s-style kitchen hadn't been upgraded much, but she liked it that way.

"It gives it character," she had once told me.

Her walls were laced with teal blue wallpaper, original white maple cabinetry, and floral drapes framing the kitchen window above the sink. Her dining table—which proudly stood in the center of the kitchen—was the only contemporary piece of furniture in the entire house. She had found it online from an artist who worked strictly with acrylics and designed custom pieces of furniture that cost way more than my 2013 Ford Escape.

I turned to Lily, who had been scrubbing the chili off the pot with her back toward me.

"Do you need help with anything?" I asked.

Turning to face me, she said, "I've got this covered. Go see Riley. He's been waiting, hun. You can't avoid him forever."

She was right. I was stalling. Riley had more patience with me than I ever could have with anyone. I made him feel uncomfortable because he accidentally made me feel uncomfortable, but still, he was willing to wait for me to lecture him about not touching me.

While giving her a forced smile and a nod, I moved toward the door that led to the backyard.

CHAPTER TWO

W hen I entered the backyard, I scanned the fence a few times before taking a step forward. My heart sped up as I walked toward the gazebo.

No one is out here but you and Riley. Relax.

Lily's low, red picket fence was surrounded by garden beds she had built a few years ago to grow her own vegetables. There was a long, stamped pathway that led to the gazebo which faced the back fence, allowing us to overlook the small man-made lake behind her property. I walked down the pathway and entered the gazebo, flipping on the lights lining the roof above us.

Riley was sitting on the bench under the gazebo, looking out toward the lake. He held his gaze, watching the bright glow of moonlight on the water's surface. Small ripples of water rolled over each other, caused by the light wind coming from the west. I sat down next to Riley and shifted my body to face in his direction.

"I'm an idiot," he blurted, standing up the moment I sat down.

I felt all his pain as he tore himself down. This was my fault, not his.

"No, you're not." I felt an overwhelming wave of guilt wash over me. Riley and I could talk about anything, and I mean anything. But in that moment, I didn't know what to say. I was upset, but also felt guilty for being upset. I was angry with myself for how I had reacted toward his touch, but also frustrated that he just wasn't getting it. I contradicted myself and I wasn't quite sure if I should even be around people anymore, especially my friends. They were going to see right through me and hate me, eventually.

"It's just a habit to touch you." The grimace on his face was too difficult for me to look at, so I turned my attention toward the lake.

"I wish it was different," I muttered. "You were the best boyfriend any girl could have. I was lucky to have you, Riley. I'm *still* lucky to have you in my life. I know I sound like a broken record when I say this, but us not being together was never your fault. None of this is about you." I held out my hand, letting him touch it. He hesitantly placed his hand on mine and I gripped it, wrapping his fingers around mine.

Breathe, Mercy. Breathe.

"I know it's not, but it's not yours either. It's hers," he said.

He didn't have to say her name. "Hers" sent a wave of panic and anxiety coursing through my veins. "She" was my worst nightmare.

He sighed and gently squeezed my hand. "You know we've been together since we were ten years old?" He paused, smiling for a brief moment, then lowered his brow. "I realize what happened to you was horrible, but you can't run away from the good in your life when bad things happen." He sat down again and looked into my eyes. "I want to take care of you. I've always wanted to take care of you."

Even under the dim lights above us, I saw how his bright blue eyes glistened with the tears that were threatening to fall from his eyes. A gust of wind blew his blond hair over his eyes and the wind tickled my cheeks, like a feather tickling the surface of my skin. I balled up the ends of my sweater and pulled it tighter over my body.

"I need to work out my own issues and I can't do it while in a relationship," I said boldly.

"You mean ... while in a relationship ... with me?" He moved his hand from mine and wiped his cheeks; the threatening tears were now rolling down slowly. He used his hoodie to dry off his fingers.

"Honestly, I don't know. But we need to start somewhere safe. Right now, being friends is safe for me," I said, turning my gaze away from him.

"I still love you," he said.

"I love you, too. You're my best friend." I stood up from the bench, unzipped my sweater, and slowly pulled the sleeves off my shoulders, until the upper part of my chest was exposed. My fingers traced along the two-inch scar on my chest.

"This reminds me of how broken I am, every single day when I wake up and see it in the mirror. It's a scar that will never go away. I don't know how to love you the way you love me, when all I see are broken pieces. God, Riley, I can't even hug my friends without feeling like my lungs are closing up."

He was the only one who knew. The only one who knew I faked every personality trait I used to have. He knew I now faked being competitive with games or caring about the next Friday night party. He knew none of that really mattered to me anymore. He also knew of how I'd coil into a lone place in my head whenever someone even lightly touched my hand.

"Does it still hurt?" he asked with genuine concern.

I shook my head. "Not physically. I know she can't hurt me anymore." I paused for a moment. "But I still have nightmares about that night."

I closed my eyes, remembering every detail from the moment I had left the graduation party at Cami's house. The party was everything I had expected. We danced until our legs turned to jelly and Riley and I had shared our last kiss. We had finally graduated, and I was looking forward to the next chapter in my life. I had left the party shortly after two in the morning, and without checking in with my mom, I hurried into my room. I was looking forward to lying down on my bed and letting my body relax. Finals that week had drained me to the point of exhaustion.

I was half-asleep, almost dreaming, but still could hear the wind tapping at my bedroom window. A creak on the floorboard startled me and I looked up, expecting to see my mom. The only light in the room was the moonlight streaming through my window.

"I'm home, Mom. Goodnight." I yawned and looked toward the door. She wasn't there.

I heard heavy breathing behind me and rolled over to the right. My mom was right next to me, on top of my bed, kneeling over my body. An object, shiny and silver, sparkled by her hip. My eyes widened when I realized what it was—a large kitchen knife.

"Close your eyes, Mercy," my mom whispered softly. "It will all be over soon."

Everything happened so fast. I don't remember the knife coming toward me, or calling 911, or even the ride in the ambulance. All I can remember is the eerie and forceful feeling of the blade slowly piercing my skin. After that, my mind completely shut down.

My own mother, who had loved me since the moment I was in the womb, had tried to kill me. They found her in our backyard, sitting in the middle of the grassy lawn, covered in my blood. She never spoke a word until her trial, when she stood before the judge and uttered these three words, "Guilty, Your Honor".

She wasn't convicted of attempted murder. My mother had hired a really good lawyer who had collected enough documentation from doctors declaring her insane. She now resides at Raven's Mental Institution in Salem, Massachusetts. It's a secure hospital where the most unstable psychopaths are sent. I was promised by the judge that she would never be set free. The thought of her escaping always made me a little nervous, though, despite his promise. We lived in

East Greenwich, Rhode Island, only ninety minutes from Salem. It is a small, quaint town where everyone knew everyone. If she showed up here, I would have no place to hide.

That thought sent a wave of panic coursing through my veins and I opened my eyes. Tears were running down my face. As I wiped them away, Riley was pulling the sweater back over my shoulders, carefully avoiding the skin near my scar. He zipped it up for me, covering the reminder that my life would never be the same.

I looked up at him with my watery eyes. "I want you to be happy, Riley. You will find someone so much better than me. I'm just too broken."

Broken, that's exactly what I am.

The thought of being best friends after dating for so long sounded ridiculous, but that's what we were. We had been boyfriend and girlfriend since before junior high. He was all I had known of a relationship. I imagined our childhood crush would turn into something intimate and mature, but it never did. I guess at such a young age, we really didn't understand love or the desires adults experience. He became my best friend, whom I occasionally kissed. We were never intimate, and rarely made out. I knew he hoped for that as we grew older, but I couldn't give him that, especially now.

His smile put me at ease. "Let's go back inside," I said.

Riley thanked Lily for the dinner and blew me a kiss. Air kisses were safe, and it was something we always did anyway, even before my attack.

"Have fun at breakfast," he said. "My work on the car shouldn't take too long. I'm pretty sure it's just a dead battery. I'll call you later." He smiled again and headed out the door.

This time, I locked the top lock and the three other bolts Lily had installed after my attack, to help me feel safer in her home.

I padded to my room and flopped down on top of my bed. I needed to clear my mind and reflect on what had happened. The following day would mark day sixty-eight since my mom had tried to kill me. That night was supposed to be a celebration with my family and friends, but it turned into a nightmare I couldn't wake up from. I needed to put all of it behind me, if I was going to survive another day.

I closed my eyes and drifted off to sleep.

Soon, the dream returned, and *he* was there again.

I never had to wonder if he would show up; he was just always there. He was the most beautiful man I had ever seen. His hair was a dark shade of brown, and it fell slightly past his shoulders. His light brown eyes were fixated on me for what felt like hours. He brushed my hair away from my eyes, gently trailing over my skin with the tips of his fingers. He tucked my long strands behind my ears, and moved his fingers down to my chin, directing my face closer to him. He kissed me intimately and I moaned before he released me. He could touch me in my dreams without me pulling away. It was refreshing to feel so alive and comfortable with someone, even if he was just a figment of my imagination.

He had been coming into my dreams for about a year now, and it felt more real than the outside world ever did. I felt safe with him. I also felt horrible that I couldn't be with Riley anymore, and yet, I wanted this dream guy in my life. I needed him in my life.

I placed my hands on his chest, slowly putting space between us. No, I didn't need a guy in my life right now. Good thing he was just my imagination that came lurking into my dreams each night.

"What are you thinking about?" he asked.

"You. I don't want this to ever change." I looked up at the dark gray clouds forming over us.

"I'll see you again tomorrow," he whispered, with a sweet smile adorning his face.

"I know." I pressed my cheek into the palm of his hand.

He lifted my chin and kissed me gently. The kiss was delicate and passionate, but only lasted a few seconds before my eyes popped open to the sound of my alarm.

CHAPTER THREE

I slapped my hand over the top of the alarm and turned it off.

"Ugh, just five more minutes," I huffed, closing my eyes again while pulling the blanket over my face.

It was slightly after ten, but it felt much earlier. The light from my bedroom window was so bright, I knew trying to go back to sleep would be impossible at this point. I grabbed my cell phone and checked my notifications. The last thing I checked were my text messages.

Cami: *Where have you been? You better be at Mario's this morning.*

Shannon: *We'll be at our usual booth at eleven.*

I hadn't seen the girls since Thursday morning's breakfast at Tippy's. It was exhausting coming up with an excuse every time they had a party or a gathering where there were people I would have to introduce myself to or make small talk with.

Cami had texted me nonstop last night trying to get me to meet her at this party thrown by our friend Landen. I decided to ignore the texts this time.

I turned away from my phone and rolled back over, snuggling my head back into my pillow. It was just a moment later when my eyes shot open as I heard Lily shouting curse words at someone. I quickly jumped up and hurried downstairs, but stopped myself when I heard my name.

"Mercy doesn't need you," she fumed to the person on the other line. She paused for a moment. "No way, that is not happening! *We* will tell her."

The floor creaked under my foot and I backed up farther behind the wall, hoping she didn't hear.

"This is your fault," she continued. "I have two weeks not only to tell her, but to prepare her. We should have told her years ago," she huffed. "Don't call here again!" She slammed the phone down and I heard her take in a few deep breaths. I had never heard Lily this upset. She was always soft-spoken and forbearing. I waited a few moments before walking in.

"Good morning," I said to her vibrantly as I walked into the pantry and grabbed a protein bar, acting like I had no idea what just went down in the kitchen.

I sat down at the kitchen table and watched as Lily fidgeted in her chair.

"Do you want some coffee?" She pointed to the coffee maker that had about a cup left in the kettle.

"I'd love some, thanks." She stood up quickly, walked over to the kettle, and poured me the remaining coffee into a mug.

When she joined me back at the table, she didn't look up.

"Sorry I haven't made breakfast yet," she apologized. I looked down to see her hands shaking.

I stared at her, waiting for her to tell me what was wrong and who was on the phone, but she just sat there, drinking her coffee with trembling hands.

"Lily?"

She looked up suddenly. "Yes?"

"Who was that on the phone?"

She hesitated, then lowered her coffee. "It was your mother."

My stomach twisted in knots. "Why? What does she want?" I asked quickly, trying to catch my breath. She had never called here. I didn't even know they let them make calls from the psychiatric ward.

She tensed and shook her head. "She wants to see you."

My mind went racing.

What could she possibly want from me? Does she want to make amends and ask for forgiveness?

I slouched back in my chair and folded my arms across my chest. "Did she say why?"

Lily looked like she was afraid to tell me something. She just stared at me with intense eyes, shaking her head. "You're not to see her," Lily ordered, clenching her jaw.

Wow, she looked pissed. Even when I had woken up in the hospital after my mom had tried to kill me, Lily only looked sad, not angry.

"Lily, I need the closure. What if she wants to tell me she's sorry? I should let her, right?" I questioned, but didn't even believe my own words. The last time I had gone to see her, she was anything but apologetic.

That day didn't just affect me, it affected Lily, too. It was right after my mom was incarcerated. I sat across a long table, staring at her for ten minutes before I had the courage to ask her the questions I desperately needed answered. While my hands shook nervously in my lap, I asked her why she wanted me dead. She stared at me with heavy eyes, clearly showing signs of distress and fatigue. She was silent, and her face showed no compassion or empathy. Her silence proved to me that she didn't care about me at all. That thought hurt worse than the feeling of a blade breaking through my sternum.

I couldn't tell if they had drugged her or if she had simply lost her mind. I wondered if there was anything going on inside her head as she looked right through me. It was in that moment of thought that she came after me like a tiger attacking its prey, leaping over the table and knocking over her chair. She lashed out at me and all I could do was shield myself with my arms, so she didn't cut my face with her sharp, unkempt nails.

Lily's voice pulled me out of my memory. "Mercy, it's not safe. You're not going, okay?"

I gave her an agreeable nod. I knew not to keep arguing with her. Lily was my guardian now and I wasn't eighteen yet. She had the right to stop me from going, but it didn't mean I wouldn't go behind her back. My mom had called for a reason. Parts of the phone call I had overheard didn't make any sense; Lily was hiding something.

She breathed in deeply and then slowly released the air from her lungs. Lily looked exhausted and worn as she shook her head and lowered her brow. "As upset as I am at what your mother did, I miss how close we all used to be." She glanced up at me. "I miss the woman she used to be."

I was so blind. Lily was hurting just as much as I was. She had lost her only sister.

We needed to focus on the good times we used to have. Talking about what my mom did only brought pain to both of us.

My favorite day with my mom was the day the city dedicated a bench to my grandfather. My uncle Joel and his husband, Derek, had flown in from New York and we were all together, laughing and crying while sharing memories of what a great man he had been.

"Remember the last photo we took as a family?" I asked her.

She sat there for a moment and then her face lit up. "Scalloptown Park!"

I was fifteen years old and the city, two years after my grandfather passed away, had dedicated a bench for him, for all his service to our community. We sat on the bench and talked about all the great memories we had with him.

"Do you still have that photo?" I asked her.

"It's on my Facebook page, I think." She grabbed her phone and scrolled through her Facebook albums for a few minutes. "There it is." She brought her phone in front of us and we looked at the picture. "I'll text it to you."

"Thanks!" I said. I needed the reminder in my phone that we were all happy and normal, once upon a time.

I looked at the photo, now in my own phone, and saved it in my picture gallery. My mom and I were sitting on that very bench with Lily, Joel, and Derek standing behind us. We'd had a jogger passing by take a quick photo.

My grandfather, William Winchester, played a huge part in our community. He was a city councilman and business owner. He owned a hotel chain here in Rhode Island and was about to expand it nationwide before he got sick.

He was only married to my nana, Helen, for ten years before she passed. Together they had three children, all a year apart from one another. The oldest was my uncle Joel, who lived in New York with his husband Derek. Their second child was my mother, Daniella, and their youngest, my aunt Lily. After my grandfather died, his inheritance was split equally between the three of them. My mom set up a trust fund for me so that when I turned eighteen, I would be able to access the money for college. I wondered if that would still happen, now that she was locked away.

Lily opened her café two years ago with her part of the money.

She had contemplated using the funds for traveling or opening a boutique, but in the end, she decided a small café was what this little town needed.

Joel was an artist and moved to New York to open a gallery of his work that he'd been creating since he was a kid. He created abstract paintings, while Derek was a photographer who focused on the real-life portraits, from *The Barber on Main Street* to *The Prostitute on 22nd Avenue*. Together, they incorporated their projects into works of art. I never had the chance to fly out there to visit them and their studio, but they often sent me photos of some of the new projects they had been working on. They agreed that after I graduated college, their spare room would be available for me to rent until I found a more permanent place to live.

Even after everything that had happened, I wasn't going to let it stop me from living my dreams. I was going to move to Providence this fall and attend Brown. I was going to work toward my bachelor's degree in marketing and someday open my own marketing firm in New York.

Lily finished up the last sip of her coffee and placed the mug in the sink. "I need to open the café. You going to be okay?" she asked.

"Yeah, I'll be fine. Will you?"

She smiled and nodded. "Have fun today."

After Lily left for the café, I took a quick shower and attached the family photo at the park in a text message for Joel.

Me: *Hey, thought you'd like a reminder of the good times. Can you visit soon?*

Joel: *I might be able to fly out for your birthday. I have a few projects I'm working on but if I can wrap them up, I'll come out. Thanks for the picture. I was thinner once. Lol.*

Me: *Dork, you aren't fat. Anyways, no problem. That would be awesome if you could come out for my birthday. Have a good one. Tell Derek I said hi.*

Joel: *Will do. Take care, kiddo.*

Closing my phone, I eyed the time once more and rushed out the door to meet my friends.

Shannon was seated at our usual table, chowing down on her pizza slice, while I joined Cami in line. Today she wore a strapless, yellow sundress reaching to her knees and flaring out at the bottom. She showed off her tall stiletto heels that defined her long, skinny legs.

"Mercy, do you want the veggie supreme?"

"Please." I nodded.

"I'll have the cheese-less veggie supreme pizza, a pepperoni and pineapple pizza, and a diet soda." She winked at the cute Mario's employee, and handed him a ten-dollar bill.

"Were you hoping he'd give us those for free?" I teased.

"Someday." She giggled, and I just rolled my eyes.

"Thanks for paying," I said while Cami smiled again at the employee and whipped her pony tail to the side. I was pretty sure I saw her throw in another wink, too.

After five minutes, they called our name, so we grabbed our pizzas and joined Shannon at our usual booth.

"Nothing like pizza for breakfast," Shannon joked.

"At least I slept in, so I didn't have to go too long on an empty stomach. My coffee has been holding me over," I explained.

"Where were you last night? I texted you like five times and then we left without you," Cami whined. "You missed a wild party ... again."

I don't think I can keep hiding this new anti-social me any longer.

Cami didn't even give me a chance to answer before she continued.

"You really should have been there. Erica hooked up with Jason Parks on one of Landen's parents' boats. It was hilarious when Landen walked in on them."

"Why is that hilarious?" I asked while flashing a crooked smile and shaking my head.

She crunched her nose at my dry response and then perked her chest up in the air. "Doesn't matter, but, where were you?"

"Binge-watched Friends so I could avoid catty gossip and pointless mingling with people we will probably never see again," I scoffed dryly.

She narrowed her eyes at me and lowered her brow. "You need more coffee."

Cami's concern about my comment faded quickly. "Who are you texting?" Cami asked Shannon, giving her a slight nudge with her elbow to pull her attention toward her.

"Riley. He just parked," Shannon answered as she removed her earphones.

Riley entered, leaped over the booth, and sat next to Cami. I turned to Riley, who immediately grabbed the menu. "Hey, did you miss the party, too?" I asked.

"I went, but it sucked." He flashed a smile, revealing his perfect white teeth and we laughed in unison.

Cami pouted as Riley ran his hands through his thick blond hair, staring back at the menu.

"I don't know why I'm looking at this menu. I get the same thing every time." We chuckled again, and he headed toward the line to order his food.

A few minutes passed and I turned my attention toward Shannon, who was focusing on her phone again, seemingly having difficulty punching the keyboard letters with her acrylic nails.

Shannon popped her head up. "Shoot. It's August 4th. We're going to see Riley's mom today, right?"

Today was the day we had planned to head up to Salem to visit Riley's mom's resting place. She had died eight years ago today, right around the time Riley asked me to be his girlfriend.

Riley was taking a seat, carrying his hot out-of-the-oven calzone. "Yeah, we can leave in an hour. I thought we could eat, fill up the gas, and then head out." He took a bite of his calzone and then washed it down with a sip of Mountain Dew.

"I need to text my mom first. I had completely forgotten. Sorry, Riley," Shannon apologized.

Riley only shrugged, still chewing his food.

Shannon's mom most likely wouldn't have an issue with her going to Salem, but I feared Lily would. Hoping she didn't protest, I sent her a text, too.

I looked around the table at my friends. I was lucky to have these three in my life. We understood each other, as each of us had broken families. After Riley's mom died, his father, who blamed himself, completely shut down to point of distancing himself from his son. Shannon was raised by her mom only, after her father walked out on them when she was only eight. Cami never knew her father, as he had been a one-night stand when Cami's mom was in college. Her mom was a drunk who chose to bring home strangers every weekend instead of finding someone to have a normal relationship with. My father had walked out when I was only one, so like Cami, I had no memory of my father. My mom claimed she wasn't in contact with him, but I had heard her several times a year since I was a child, talking on the phone with someone, arguing over me. The phone calls stopped about a year ago.

I looked down at my phone and Lily still hadn't responded to my text. I knew going to Salem made her nervous, but it wasn't like my mom was going to know I was there.

CHAPTER FOUR

W e arrived at St. Peter's Cemetery around one thirty. This graveyard was one of the largest and oldest in Salem; we passed a tomb that dated all the way back to 1673. It was still well maintained with gorgeous landscape and lush greenery. Karen was born right outside of Salem and told Mr. Davis that this was where she wanted to be buried, even though it wasn't near where they lived. Riley and his father came here every year, but once Riley got his driver's license, Riley's father stopped coming. That's when we started coming with him.

"Here, guys." Riley handed each of us a red rose to place on the ground in front of the tomb. We walked slowly and quietly toward her stone. It was beautiful. It read "Beloved Wife, Mother, Friend & Nurse" right below her name.

"I miss you, Karen." I placed my rose on the ground.

After a few minutes of silence, Cami spoke up. "Why don't you say something about her, Riley?"

Riley looked around at us. We locked eyes and Riley knelt next to the tomb with a red rose still in his hand.

"It took me several years after she died to not blame my dad or myself for not seeing how much she had been hurting. It had to have been a lot for her to take her own life and leave us the way she did. My dad still blames himself, probably blames me, too."

"Riley, he doesn't blame you," I said as I knelt next to him. "Your father loves you. He just hasn't healed."

He closed his eyes and knitted his brows together. I hesitantly placed my hand on his back. Touching others wasn't as hard for me, it was being touched that I struggled with, though I preferred to fully separate myself from human contact, if at all possible. I wasn't going to let my being uncomfortable stop me from comforting him today, so I dealt with it.

"I miss you, Mom," he said, as if she were somewhere near, listening to us.

His fingers lightly touched the carving on the stone, lingering by her name.

I backed away and we waited for him to release his hand from the tomb. He turned toward us, opening his mouth to speak again, but halted when we heard a loud screech coming from an old mausoleum behind us.

I turned my head quickly to look while Cami and Shannon jumped back slightly.

"What the hell was that?" I asked.

Shannon took a step in the direction of the sound. "It sounded like two cinderblocks grinding across each other." She signaled in the direction heading toward the back of the cemetery.

"Um, yeah, we need to go. I hate this," Cami whined. Cami was never thrilled when it came to anything remotely scary. She wouldn't even watch the animated *The Nightmare Before Christmas*, because the Boogie Man scared her too much.

"It's coming from that mausoleum." Riley pointed in its direction.

"It kind of sounded like a coffin sliding open," Shannon teased.

Cami stuck her tongue out at her.

We heard the screech again, but this time it was much louder, causing Cami to jump again.

After my attack, and my recent paranoia that someone had been watching me, you'd think something like this would have me running for the car, but it didn't. Despite my issues, I felt strangely compelled to investigate the sound.

"I'm going to go check it out," I said, turning to Shannon. "Are you coming with?"

"You're crazy, Mercy," Cami cried.

"Of course I'll come." Shannon beamed as she looked at Riley.

"Naw, I'll stay here with Cami." His smirk made Cami smile and her shoulders relaxed.

As Shannon and I walked toward the mausoleum, we heard Cami shout to us, "It's probably a ghost!"

When we arrived at the front of the tall mausoleum, I pulled on the handle, but it wouldn't open. Shannon placed her ear against the door as another screech echoed inside. I joined her to listen and the moment my ear touched the wall, a loud thump shot me off my feet and I stumbled over a raised tomb behind me. She caught me before I hit the ground. Instantly, I tensed, brushing her hands away nonchalantly and trying not to make it obvious how much I hated being grabbed like that, regardless of whether she was just helping.

"Whoa. Are you okay?" she asked, panic rising in her voice.

"I'm fine." I wasn't fine. Something sharp had scratched the back of my leg during the fall. I looked down and blood was oozing out of the scratch on my calf. Without tending to it and pointing it out to her, I moved back over to the wall of the mausoleum and placed my ear against the grainy concrete.

"What happened? What is it?" Cami shouted again from a distance.

Shannon signaled a thumbs up and she joined me at the wall again. We stood there for another five minutes, but the noise had stopped. I glanced above the door and there wasn't a name of the person on it like most of the mausoleums. I turned to Shannon, who still had her ear up to the door.

"Maybe no one is buried inside," I suggested as I put my hand on the handle again, trying one more time.

"It's locked. Mercy, let's go."

I couldn't shake the thought that someone was inside.

"Okay. Okay," I agreed.

We walked back to Cami and Riley, and Cami had her arm linked around Riley's arm for comfort. "I want to go. Cemeteries freak me out," Cami complained when we approached.

She looked at Riley, waiting for a response.

"Yeah, let's go," he said.

I took one last glance toward the mausoleum.

BANG!

The loud crash came back, but louder and fiercer. We all jumped backward again and Cami was already running to the car.

"Okay," I said quickly. "Time to go."

We stopped at a few checkpoints on the way home to take photos together and swung by a bookstore in Providence. It was almost six by the time we left the bookstore.

Riley dropped the girls off at their homes, then dropped me off last. I wasn't looking forward to facing Lily, who still hadn't responded since I had texted her this morning.

When I walked in the door, she was sitting at the table with a glass of wine and half-eaten lasagna she had made for one.

I minced toward the table cautiously, waiting to be yelled at.

"Hey," I said while taking a seat at the table.

"How's Riley?" she asked, but I knew that wasn't the question she wanted to ask me.

"I didn't go see my mom, if that's what you're wondering. We only went for Riley."

She let out a sigh. "That's good." She smiled, but then nervously tapped her fingers on the table. "So, I was thinking we can go out to dinner this Saturday night, just the two of us. There are some things I'd like to talk to you about afterward. It can also be like your early birthday dinner. Anywhere you want to go."

"Okay, I'd like that," I said, but I noticed Lily still looked nervous. I was pretty sure this dinner was to discuss what she and my mom had talked about over the phone.

After our chat, she went upstairs with her wine glass. I didn't bother getting ready for bed. I laid my head on my pillow and closed my eyes after a long, exhausting day. Moments after my mind drifted into my dream, I felt his hands gently caressing my neck. His soft lips reached my collar bone and tickled my skin, creating a mountain of goosebumps up my back.

"I've missed you," he breathed, stroking my cheek with the back of his fingers. I moaned at his touch and placed my hand over his, stretching out his fingers and leaning into his palm.

"I've missed you, too."

He grinned and kissed me gently. "Now, tell me about your day."

CHAPTER FIVE

A fter my last dream, he made shorter appearances when I closed my eyes at night.

Why did he disappear the moment I touched him?

On Wednesday, he had been in my dream for just a brief moment, and then he had disappeared right in front of me, leaving me alone in a dark and empty room. By the following Friday night, he was nowhere to be found. I panicked; this wasn't my usual dream. It was as if he were trying to reach me, but something was pulling him away.

My dream tonight was different. I was surrounded by beautiful, vibrant green trees with thick brown trunks. Right in front of me, the leaves transformed from green, to red and a few shades of amber. They suddenly disappeared and I was left with dead, leafless branches. There was one tree that stood out among the others. Dark red leaves fell slowly from its branches onto the ground. I was hypnotized by its beauty.

A gray, smoky mist crept through the trees and then wrapped around my body. I walked forward as each of the leaves dripped what looked like thick red liquid.

Is this blood?

The liquid turned from red to black, swirling clockwise, and becoming thicker and thicker like molten lava, making it harder for me to walk as it closed in around my body.

I looked ahead and there stood a mausoleum, like the one at the cemetery. I was finally able to lift my legs from the thick lava and move forward, and as I approached the entryway, my legs gave way and I stumbled through the door.

I stood up and brushed the remaining thick liquid off my pants. I walked toward a coffin that sat at the center of the room and approached cautiously. The lid was opened slightly, and I peered inside, expecting to see the dead figure of a rotting corpse.

What I saw instead was a secret passageway that led down into a dark tunnel. Wrought iron stairs were hooked to the top of the coffin, but I couldn't see how far down they went. I lifted myself up to look deeper inside, but before I could peer all the way in, I felt a force grabbing me by the neck and pushing my body forward and into the coffin. I was nearing the bottom of the tunnel when my eyes shot open to the light coming in from my bedroom window.

What the hell was that?

I looked at the clock and noticed I had slept through my alarm. I stood up from my bed, but my legs felt fatigued, as if I had really journeyed somewhere in my dream. Sweat covered my forehead and I wiped it off with my top sheet. My body was shaking slightly from the adrenaline rush and I had to take a few deep breaths in to steady my breathing.

It was just a dream, Mercy. Don't need to panic.

I took a quick shower and pulled my hair back into a wet ponytail. Lily opened the shop late on Saturday mornings and extended the café hours into lunch, so she was still in the kitchen brewing coffee.

Entering the kitchen, I inhaled the scent of Lily's homemade blueberry waffles.

"Hey, Mercy. Before you head out to do whatever it is you have planned for today, I have something for you."

I had made plans with Cami and Shannon to head to Goddard Park for a breakfast picnic and then hop on over to Main to check out a dress shop for Shannon. Her cousin was getting married in Vermont in a few weeks and she was her Maid of Honor.

I grabbed one of her blueberry waffles and sat down at the table, eating it without a plate or fork. "What is it?" I asked, my mouth stuffed with the bite of the waffle.

"I know your birthday isn't for another two weeks, but I wanted to give you your gift early."

She held her hand out and dangled a black stone necklace from her fingers.

I took the necklace from her and stared at the stone. It was enchanting.

"It's beautiful. Where did you get it?" I stared, mesmerized.

"It's a family heirloom that gets passed down to each firstborn female in our bloodline. This was your mother's and she had planned to give it to you right before your eighteenth birthday. Please accept it as a gift, from me. I made it into a necklace for you."

"It's so pretty." I looked more closely at the stone and turned it around. Carved into the back of the stone was a pentagram. "A pentagram?" I asked.

"It's a jet stone and that is our family crest."

"A pentagram?" I asked again.

She smirked. "We are descendants of Salem witches, after all." She pointed to the symbol on the necklace. "It was more than just a symbol of witchcraft, Mercy. It meant something to our family back then. They believed it protected them."

She touched each point of the pentagram gingerly. "Each point of the pentagram represents a different universal element: Earth, Air,

Water, and Fire." Her fingers then lingered on the top point of the star. "And Spirit." She leaned back into her chair. "History books spoke of the witches of Salem being able to harness powers drawn from those elements. Without the elements, there'd be no power within them."

I snickered. "A little deep for this early in the morning, Lily." I looked back down at the necklace. "You really believe in this." It was a statement, not a question.

"We all should believe in something, Mercy." She wasn't smiling.

Is she serious?

I placed the necklace on the table and stood up. "I gotta go. Thanks for the necklace," I said dryly.

She immediately picked it up, grabbed my hand, and placed the necklace in my palm. "Wear it, Mercy. It's from me, not her."

I sighed, looked at the necklace again, and fastened it around my neck. "Thank you, Lily," I said warmly. I knew she was doing what she felt was best for me, even though taking something my mom intended to give felt weird.

She perked up. "Are we still on for dinner tonight?"

"Yeah, I was thinking maybe we can eat somewhere we haven't been to in a while, like La Masseria? I know you love their wine," I teased.

She rolled her eyes at me, finally smiling. "Sounds good, just be home at six and we can leave by then." She handed me my keys which were hanging on the hook near the door. "Have fun today."

I stepped out onto the porch and breathed in the scent of Lily's lavender plants. The wind picked up, threatening a storm, which we were expecting in the next few hours. The beautiful leaves reached for each other as pieces of them broke off the branches and fell onto the street.

Once in the car, I turned on the radio, settled for the local rock station and sang along to *Forfeit* by Chevelle.

I focused straight ahead on the road, narrowing my eyes on the white lines in the center of the two lanes. Maybe I should have had a cup of Lily's coffee she was brewing this morning. My mind was zoning out while counting each line as I drove past them, as if I were on autopilot.

I was about to turn on Howland Drive when an animal ran in front my car so fast, I couldn't quite make out what it was, but the distraction was enough that I swerved into the left lane and slammed on my brakes. The wheels turned sharply to the right, but this only caused my car to spin around in circles, throwing me into the steering wheel and then up against the window, smashing my head violently against the glass. Then, blackness.

When I woke up, my car was at the bottom of a ditch on the side of the road. I looked around and the only way I could see to get out of the car was through the shattered window. I felt the warmth of the blood pumping from my forehead and dripping over my left eye.

I looked through the window, assessing my environment, trying to figure out where I was, or if there were any passersby I could call out to. My car was on its left side, leaning against a small tree that I had nearly knocked down. I tried to move, but it was no use. My left leg was lodged between the dashboard and my seat. My ankle was stuck, and I thought about moving it slightly back and forth to wiggle out of my shoe. I was about to move it when I felt a sudden surge of excruciating pain shoot up my leg. A closer examination revealed that a cracked piece of plastic from the dashboard had pierced into my calf.

Oh my God!

"Help!" I screamed as loudly as I could. "Help me! Someone help me!"

No response.

My head was spinning and my heart raced. My lungs suddenly felt clogged and I found myself desperately gasping for air.

Breathe, Mercy. Breathe.

I tried again to move my leg out of its stuck position; I heard a snap in my ankle.

"Shit!" Tears stung my eyes. "This is not happening." My body ached from head to toe and I felt that any minute now, I was going to pass out from the amount of blood I felt pouring out of my leg.

With a broken ankle and bloody calf, I managed to pull my leg from under the dashboard, but the pain from moving it only made me cry out more.

I tried to relax and not panic, but the pain didn't subside. Time was ticking, and here I was, stranded, hurt, helpless, and all alone. Finally, I heard movements from behind the car, but when I looked around, I saw no one.

"Who's there?" I cried out.

No response. A deep sadness overcame me as I realized I was alone out here, but then I heard something.

The door flew off my car and just like that, it was gone.

What on earth is going on?

A man's muscular arms reached down and pulled the piece of plastic out of my leg. For a second, I thought I was going to pass out.

I forced myself to look over at the man, but all I could see was his chiseled chest as he wrapped his arms around my waist and hoisted me out of my seat, cradling me in his arms. Looking down at his arm, I noticed a flame-shaped tattoo above his right wrist. Strangely, I didn't flinch when he touched me. The stranger laid me gently on the ground, releasing his hold on me

I still hadn't looked up at my hero. "Thank you for helping me," I said weakly.

"Why aren't you healing?" His voice was calm and steady.

I looked up, confused, but in an instant, he was gone.

My head was pounding so hard, I was forced to close my eyes and lie all the way down on the ground. My mind went black again and into the darkness of my dreams.

I was relieved to not feel pain from my leg and ankle anymore, but everything around me felt suffocating. I tried to take a few breaths, but my lungs were restricted.

I walked a few feet till I entered a clearing where a woman with a rope wrapped around her neck was standing on a ladder below a large tree. The rope was secured to a thick branch above her. There was no escape for her; only certain death. When I looked more closely at this girl, I noticed that her face was the same as mine, but she had long red hair and she was wearing clothes no one would wear today. An angry crowd surrounded the girl, hoisting up flaming torches.

"Witch!" they chanted in unison.

"Hang her now!" a man bellowed.

The girl closed her eyes, as the ladder was kicked out under her. Her feet dropped and her body went limp. The shock of her death made me scream, closing my eyes tightly, no longer able to tolerate the sight of watching someone die. When I opened my eyes again, all I saw was a white-painted ceiling above me.

CHAPTER SIX

"Oh thank goodness, Mercy," Lily whispered. "Shannon, please go tell the nurse she's awake."

I was lying in a hospital bed, wearing nothing but a flimsy hospital gown and a plastic band around my wrist.

Lily grabbed my hand and I flinched. She must have noticed it this time because her face looked wary. "You're safe in the hospital. It's me, Lily."

I felt achy, but the pain I felt wasn't nearly as painful as it had been in the car.

They must have me on some pretty strong painkillers.

I looked down at my leg and noticed my ankle wasn't in a cast, either. I placed my fingertips on my forehead, gliding them across the skin ever so gently, but felt nothing.

What the hell?

I looked up at Lily, "What happened?"

"Someone saw your car from their house across the street and called 911. Before the ambulance reached you, they saw you walking into the woods and then collapse about twenty feet from your car. You must have passed out," she explained.

"I was walking?" I shook my head. "No, I remember. I broke my ankle."

I tried to recall what had happened, but my mind wasn't making sense of it.

Lily and Riley looked at each other and then back to me. I glanced down at my foot, moving my ankle from side to side. "Or, I thought I did."

"From what the nurses have said, you didn't break anything," Riley added. "Kind of surprised though, your car was a wreck. Your door had been completely ripped off in the crash."

Ah ha! I didn't imagine this. My door was indeed ripped off by someone. Ugh, but could a man actually do that?

"Where's Cami?" I asked Lily.

"She's here, somewhere. She was in the waiting room the last time I saw her, talking to her mom on the phone."

Before Lily opened her mouth again, Shannon walked in with the nurse who checked my monitors.

"Your doctor will be right in," the nurse assured me.

I shifted my body toward Riley. "Hey, you," I said to him, who was within arm's reach. I shot him a weak smile and he reciprocated.

"I was worried about you," he admitted, placing his hand by my arm, but not touching me.

"I needed you here. Thank you." I moved my hand over to his and lightly touched his fingers.

After a few seconds, I removed my fingers from his and looked over at my aunt. "Lily, I'm so sorry about the car. I may need to borrow your beater truck for a while." I laughed at my joke.

"Ha, it's not that bad. I need someone to drive it every now and then anyway." She laughed with me and leaned back against her chair. "What do you remember from the accident?"

"An animal ran across the street. I didn't have time to avoid it, so I swerved off the road and into the forest. Then this man came and pulled me from the car."

I thought about how he'd appeared and disappeared so quickly.

How could he have just left me alone like that? He was right there, holding me, comforting me. And then he was gone. But he had said something to me first. What was it again?

"There wasn't a man, Mercy. They found you there alone," Lily explained.

As I tried to make sense of everything ... tried to figure out what was real and what wasn't ... a doctor entered the room.

"Glad to see you're awake," the doctor said as he walked in. "I'm Doctor Reid. How are you feeling?" he asked.

I looked down at my ankle again. "No broken ankle or large wound on my leg?"

"I examined you myself. There's a small wound on your calf and your forehead, but aside from that, you're fine," he explained.

This isn't possible.

"Please check my ankle." I looked at him nervously.

Was I losing my mind?

Doctor Reid pulled a chair to the end of the bed and lifted the blanket. He placed his hands on my ankle gently and moved it slightly right.

"Does that hurt?" he asked.

I shook my head.

He turned it to the left. "How about that?"

I shook my head again. There was no pain, not even a little bit.

"Is it possible, when you were passed out, that you dreamed you broke it?" he asked.

"It's possible," I replied, thinking about his theory. It made more sense than a broken ankle healing itself within an hour.

"The only real concern I have is that you did pass out at the scene, so I'd like to keep you here for twenty-four hours, just to monitor you. After you head home tomorrow, just take it easy. If you pass out again or get headaches, call my office and I'll refer you to a neurologist," he instructed.

"Maybe you fell asleep at the wheel?" Shannon, who had been sitting quietly in the back of the room, finally joined in.

Her theory made sense too. I remembered zoning out and feeling so tired. Maybe there hadn't been an animal. Maybe instead I simply fell asleep, crashed my car, and dreamed everything after that.

"Mercy, I'll stay here as long as you need. I can keep the café closed for the rest of the day," she told me.

I shook my head. "No, please don't do that. Like the doctor said, I'm fine. It's just routine monitoring." I looked up at Shannon and Riley. "Thanks for coming, guys."

Shannon opened her mouth to say something, right as Cami barged through the door. "Oh my God, Mercy!"

I rolled my eyes and giggled. "It's not serious, Cami. I'm fine. They just want to keep me here overnight."

"Well, that doesn't sound like you're fine," she huffed.

"How's your mom?" I asked, changing the focus away from me.

She frowned and shook her head. "I should probably get back to her. She's having a bad day."

"You guys are amazing for being here." I turned to Riley. "I'll text you later."

A few hours after everyone had left the hospital, I was getting restless. Once I climbed out of the bed, the sudden urge to pee took over.

After relieving myself, I washed my hands and looked up at the mirror. I brought my hands to my forehead and pulled the bandage back to reveal ... nothing.

What?

My heart raced. There wasn't a cut on my forehead, only a light pink smudge from the blood soaked on the Band-Aid. I looked down at my leg where the piece of plastic from the car had been lodged, pulled the bandage off, and there was no gash there, either. When I grabbed my pants from the hospital bag, I noticed a two-inch hole right where the plastic had been. Turning my pants inside out, I saw what the nurses must not have noticed.

Blood. A lot of blood.

No, I didn't dream this. The amount of blood on my pants was something that could only come from a deep laceration. Something was happening to me, something strange.

Me: *I'm going crazy in this hospital bed.*

Shannon: *You're home tomorrow. You feeling okay?*

Me: *I feel fine and they still won't let me leave.*

Shannon: *I'm pretty sure you're not a prisoner.*

Me: *You're no fun. BUST ME OUT!*

Shannon: *LOL, I always told you I'd have your back if you got in a jam.*

Riley: *Ladies, I'm trying to sleep. Send each other a separate text, please.*

Cami: *Hi guys, I need to sleep, too. It's almost midnight.*

Me: *All right. All right. Call you guys tomorrow.*

I closed my phone and rolled over. I shut my eyes but couldn't fall asleep. Hospital beds were awful. I turned back around and sat up. When I pressed the bed controls to sit upright, there was a noise coming from the door.

Click. It was a soft rattle from the doorknob.

The handle turned to the left and then stopped. I sat there waiting for the on-call nurse to come in, but she didn't. I stood up from my bed and waited again.

I gulped.

You're just being paranoid, Mercy. You are safe in a hospital. A nurse just changed their mind on coming in.

Even though that was the rational explanation, my heartbeat picked up.

To put my nerves at ease, I walked to the door and opened it. I looked down the hall and the only hospital employee was a female nurse sitting at the desk from a distance, looking at a computer monitor.

"Excuse me," I said as I approached her.

"Hi, Mercy. How can I help you?"

"Yes ... um ... did you just try and come inside my room?"

She looked slightly concerned. "No. I've been sitting here for at least thirty minutes."

"Oh ... well, okay. Goodnight," I said but I didn't move. "Is there any other nurse working right now on this floor?"

She shook her head. "Just me." She stood up and walked on the other side of the desk. "I'll walk you back to your room."

She escorted me back. Climbing into my bed, she helped my legs up, even though I didn't need help. "If you need anything, please let me know."

"Okay, thank you." I rolled back over, while listening to the sound of the door closing.

Once I heard her footsteps continue down the hall, my pulse picked up again. No one else was in the room, but a sense of foreboding washed over me.

CHAPTER SEVEN

It was eleven when I finished my shower and grabbed my belongings. Lily would be here any minute to pick me up. I grabbed my phone and found Riley's name.

Me: *Finally getting out of here. Did you guys end up going somewhere after you left?*

Riley: *Shannon and Cami went home and I went down to Ted's Bar and Grill to play a few rounds of pool with Jeff.*

Me: *Sounds more fun than my night. I don't think I can spend any more time indoors. Want to meet up later?*

Riley: *Yeah, I'm down, let's go to Goddard Park. I'll grab Taco Bell on the way.*

Me: *Perfect, let's meet around two. I'll wait till Lily goes back to the café. There's no way she'd let me go anywhere after just getting back from the hospital.*

Riley: *Sounds like a plan, see you soon.*

We lived about ten minutes from Goddard Park. Lily dropped me off at the house, and after she left to go back to the café, I grabbed the keys to her truck and drove to meet Riley.

When I arrived at the marina, Riley was already sitting on a bench facing the rippling waves from the water in the cove.

Goddard Park was one of my favorite places near East Greenwich. The park stretched across four hundred acres along the Greenwich Cove. There were beautiful trails, canoeing, places to picnic, and most of the time my friends and I just came here to look out over the water and talk. It was peaceful, and it allowed us to escape a little bit from the chaos in our lives.

"I love this place," I stated as I approached.

"It's gorgeous," he replied. He turned around and held out his hand. "Two plain bean burritos for you. Extra packets of mild sauce."

I sat down next to him. "Thank you. That hospital food was awful."

After we finished our lunch, I looked at Riley, whose face turned grim.

"Are you doing okay, Riley?" I asked.

He glanced at me and then back to the water. "Life is really hard for me right now, Mercy," he confessed. "How do we go every day without breaking down?" He ran his hand through his hair. "Remember how my dad and I used to come out here when my mom was still alive and fish on our little paddle boat?"

I nodded. "Yeah, I remember. Your dad was so excited when you caught your first fish, he cooked it up that night. He didn't realize my mom and I didn't eat fish, but he tried to serve us what you guys caught that day, anyway." We both giggled at the memory.

His laughter slowly faded and he looked back out at the water. "I just come out here now by myself. I was on my way to fish yesterday morning before I got the call about your accident. I was coming here ... to fish alone."

He pointed to a group of trees on our left that were farther into the water than the rest. I saw a few wooden paddle boats from a distance tied to a tree that reached over the water.

"There isn't an official dock on this side, so people just keep their boats tied to the trees. I'm pretty sure strangers have taken ours out before." He laughed, but I couldn't join his laughter. I hurt for him.

Riley had been alone for so many years; there was so much sadness in his eyes, and I didn't see it until now. I had been his girlfriend and never noticed the pain he felt from the absence of his father's love. He must have felt me pulling away from him this past year, way before what happened with my mom. I saw that now. He hadn't had a father to give him affection, he'd had me, and now I had taken that from him.

We sat on the bench, looking over the water for what felt like an hour or so, staring at the waves and sharing some of the good times from this past year at school. I looked at my phone. It was nearly four and I knew I needed to head home soon before Lily got back.

"I should get home. Lily usually gets back around five." I turned to him and held out my hand. "Will you hold my hand?" He looked down at my hand, hesitated, and then placed his fingers in mine. My stomach was in knots and I drew in a deep breath. "I don't know why this is so hard. You didn't hurt me." I closed my eyes and tears spilled over my cheeks. "But don't let go."

He gripped my hand tighter and I finally relaxed.

He held my hand a few minutes longer and then I let go, releasing our touch. "Okay," I said as I stood up. "We should go."

When we were both in our cars, I waved at him and turned the key. Lily's truck stood still. "Oh, you crappy beater truck, don't do this." I tried again, and nothing happened. I opened the door to flag

Riley down, but he was already driving off. Waving my hands in the air frantically, I had hoped he'd see me in his rearview mirror, but he didn't. He turned the corner and was gone. I ran to the car to grab my phone, hoping I could get him to come back for me, but didn't see it anywhere. I looked in my purse and under the seat.

"Dammit," I swore out loud.

Back at the bench where we had been sitting, I looked for where I would have put my phone or dropped it.

Ugh, where are you, phone?

I looked around and no one else was at the park. If I could just flag someone down who was going for a walk, I could maybe use theirs to call Riley.

Seriously, where is my phone? I just had it.

"Are you looking for this?" A low voice asked from behind me. It startled me and I yelped, turning around and taking a few steps back.

It was a guy. A really hot guy!

Despite his good looks, his appearance didn't settle my nerves one bit. He was a stranger that had come out of nowhere. His dark, wavy brown hair reached the center of his neck, messy but perfect at the same time. His five o'clock shadow was just the right amount of scruff to complement his perfectly high cheekbones and strong jawline. The feature that stood out the most were his amber eyes. They were breathtaking. I had never seen anyone with amber eyes before. For a brief moment, as his eyes looked into mine, a sense of familiarity hit me.

Do I know him? No. I would have recognized that face.

"Yes ... thank you," I answered with shaky breath. I looked around the park to see if anyone else was around. We were alone.

"Here." He held out my phone. I stretched out my hand and grabbed it, putting it in my back pocket. The stranger was wearing dark jeans and a brown T-shirt with a maroon hoodie zipped halfway up. The hoodie was snug against his arms, and I imagined for a brief moment what he looked like under his shirt. I tried to clear my thoughts, so I could focus.

He's a stranger, Mercy, and you're alone. Please don't murder me.

"Do you have a name?" he asked.

Do not give him your real name.

"Angie ..."

"Caleb Blackwell. Nice to meet you, Angie." He stepped closer to me and held out his hand.

I shook his hand. He held on, probably feeling the sweat of my palms and slight tremble that was picking up the longer he held it.

Why is he not letting go?

"You're shaking," he said with a sideways grin on his face. He finally let go of my hand.

"I need to go. Thanks for finding my phone." I stepped quickly to the side to walk by him, but he moved into my path, blocking me from going any further.

"Mercy, relax. I'm not going to hurt you."

Everything around me froze in place and my heart stopped in its tracks.

He knows me. How did he know my real name?

I found myself hyperventilating as I took a step back.

"Did you ... did you go ... go to my school?"

Act like you're not scared out of your freaking mind, Mercy.

"I don't understand. How do you know my name?"

"We met a long time ago, but your memory of me no longer exists. I tracked you down tonight and was waiting for you to be alone after that boy left."

"Did you mess with my car?" I asked. Tears welled up in my eyes and I couldn't stop the uncontrollable shaking.

He didn't answer. His intense gaze was fixated on me, as if he had been analyzing every detail of my face.

This time I stepped back, thinking if I ran fast enough, I could run from behind the bench and get to my car before he could stop me. It was as if he could read my thoughts; he moved forward, grabbed my arm in a tight grip and pulled me toward his chest. He looked down at me, brushing the hair away from my eyes and tucking it behind my ears.

"I've missed you," he said softly as he slowly lowered me down to the bench again next to us.

Oh my God, he's crazy.

The look he gave me—as if I meant something to him—shook me to the core.

"Please don't hurt me." I closed my eyes as if I were anticipating a blow. Tears stung my eyes.

"I already told you, I'm not going to hurt you." I heard a frustrated grunt and sigh come from him. "Open your eyes, Mercy, and look at me."

My eyes shot open.

"You're in danger and it's not from me. Someone has been following you. I'm here to protect you." He slowly released his grip and gave us some space.

"I don't want your help. I don't know you." My voice cracked.

Oh God, Riley. Please come back.

He let out another frustrated grunt. "Mercy, you really need to relax and trust me. I know it's hard, but I am the only one you can trust right now." I couldn't believe what he was saying. He was a stalker and I had to get away from him. He must have seen me eyeing my car, because he gripped my wrist again, keeping me from moving.

"Now, we can chat out here, or we can drive over to the other side of the cove and talk over coffee. I say coffee."

"I ... I ..."

"Look, I knew if I approached you with Lily or your friends around, there'd be more questions than answers I'm willing to give them. This is the first time I've been able to get you alone. Now, let's get in my car and drive to the other side where the bar is. You can come willingly, or I can make you."

Screw this guy.

I bent down quickly, grabbed a long, thick branch, and brought it hard against his head. He fell to the ground, so I bolted toward the forest.

I didn't get far before I felt my body lunge forward and my legs kick back. His grip on my ankle caused me to wince.

"Mercy, stop running, dammit. I can explain everything if you just stop freaking the hell out."

I kicked him in the face with my other leg until he let go and I got back to my feet, now sprinting deeper into the forest.

Where am I going to go?

All I knew was this guy was not someone I wanted to be alone with. I may not have seen anyone else out there, but I hoped someone would hear me and help me.

"Help!" I screamed as loud as I could. I just needed to lock myself in the truck and call the police.

When I turned around, he was nowhere to be seen. A heavy sigh escaped as I eyed Lily's truck about a hundred feet ahead. I looked around one more time and then sprinted to the truck. Once inside, I locked it and pulled my phone out of my pocket. My phone had been turned off.

This is going to take too long.

He would reach me before my phone powered on. I powered it on anyway and put my hands back on the keys which were still in the ignition. I tried again. The car didn't make a sound.

Please turn on, please turn on.

I gripped the keys so tightly that the house key was digging into my palm. "Turn on!" The feeling of electricity sparked in my hand, followed by a green light from my fingertips. I quickly removed my hand and the car started up.

What the hell?

The shock of what had just happened stunned me. I couldn't move or think straight.

I sensed movement ahead coming out of the forest and I looked up. He was standing there. His sleeves were now pulled up to his elbows, revealing his muscular arms. My eyes narrowed down to his wrist, revealing a red flame tattoo that reached from his wrist to his elbow. My stomach churned and I felt like throwing up. It was him; it was the man who had pulled me from my car after the accident.

CHAPTER EIGHT

I knew I should have driven straight to the cops, but I didn't. I was too scared to stop. After about an hour of driving around, making sure he wasn't tailing me, I pulled into my driveway and ran into the house, screaming for Lily.

She bolted down the stairs, catching herself on the railing as she missed a couple steps, and ran into the kitchen. She must have seen the mascara smudged all over my face and the scrapes I now had from the being chased and attacked by my stalker. Fear was the only expression on her face.

I told Lily what had happened and of course she was more concerned with my safety than the fact that I left with her truck so soon after my accident.

She called the police and they arrived at the house to take my statement. They asked me to come to the police station the next day to give a description of him to a sketch artist.

"We'll find him, ma'am," Officer Bolton assured me. I knew there was no way they could guarantee that, though.

Who knows how long this guy had been watching me or how long he planned to play this game? He also wasn't what I pictured a stalker would look like, that's for sure. He was handsome and charming, but then again, the devil himself was the master of deception.

I sat next to Lily and nodded when the officer asked me questions. I did my best to explain what had happened and I even mentioned the incident during my accident the day before. I mentioned to the officer that I had seen someone watching me a few times this week, and about the incident at the hospital. Lily told me how sorry she was for not believing me. I left out the part about what happened with my hands at the park. I didn't believe it myself.

Did I really start the car with some green glow from my hands? That isn't even possible. Things like that don't exist.

After the police left, I sat down with Lily at the kitchen table. "It was the same guy who pulled me from the car. It wasn't a dream."

"You're not to be alone, okay? I will make sure we have the same work shift so you don't have to open the café by yourself." Lily grabbed a new bottle of wine from the cabinet and popped off the cork, slowly pouring her wine of choice, Cabernet Sauvignon, into her glass.

Lily sat back down at the table and I shook my head. "I can't make you change your schedule for me," I said.

"Are you kidding me? My job as your legal guardian is to protect you. Once we close shop, have Riley or someone pick you up and stay with them until I can get home. The paperwork and accounting won't take me more than an hour." She placed her hand near mine, which was resting on the table. "They'll find him, okay? We will go to the police station tomorrow morning so you can give the sketch artist a description."

I stood up and walked over to my phone that had been charging. I unhooked my phone from the charger, walked toward the stairs and turned to Lily. "I need to sleep. Can we talk about this in the morning?"

"Of course we can. Get some rest." She walked up to me and

grabbed my hand, squeezing it softly. I didn't pull away. I didn't flinch or feel uneasy.

This is good. I feel safe.

I squeezed her hand back and gave her a warm smile. "Night, Lily."

When I entered my room, I plugged my phone into the charger again, set it on my nightstand, and pulled out my pajamas from my drawer.

Ugh, I probably look like hell.

I removed my clothes by my bed and tossed them into the hamper in the corner of my room. I smelled so bad after today that I couldn't just crawl into bed, so I decided a much-needed shower was in order. Entering the bathroom, I grabbed the hooks to my necklace but then stopped, now glancing up at the mirror. My heart leaped out of my chest. The only messes on my body were a few twigs and dirt from when I fell in the forest. I turned around to view my backside and saw nothing. I examined every part of me, but my skin was flawless, just like what I had witnessed at the hospital.

"How is it possible?" I asked out loud, still not believing what I was seeing in the mirror.

"Magic," a familiar voice calmly spoke behind me.

I screamed and jumped back, banging my back against the towel rack. I winced but didn't take my eyes off him. It was *him*, standing in my bathroom doorway. I quickly covered my chest, standing there in all my nakedness. He had a grin on his face, but kept his eyes locked on mine. I quickly grabbed the towel off the hook next to me and covered myself up again.

"Lily!" I screamed so loudly I probably popped a blood vessel in my eye.

"She won't hear you. I put up a shield around your room." He kept his eyes focused on mine.

"A shield? What are you talking about, you freak?" I shouted.

I backed up another foot, but closer to the shower, and looked around for anything that could be used as a weapon. I grabbed a soap dispenser from the counter and threw it toward his head, but he only moved to the side, letting it land on the floor behind him.

He huffed and shook his head. "Really, Mercy?"

I screamed Lily's name again.

Caleb lifted his left hand and pointed to the walls that I now noticed were radiating with a blue glow. My jaw dropped open.

"Go ahead. Put your hand on it."

I blinked at him and then looked back at the blue light. I placed my fingers on the light and felt a surge of energy push my hand back lightly, but I was still able to linger my fingertips on the surface of the light. The light grew brighter the longer my fingers were on it. The inexplicable sight in front of me defied all laws of physics.

"That shield is around your entire room. You can't leave, no one can come in, and no one can hear us."

My heartbeat picked up, creating an unnerving feeling in my stomach.

"What are you? How are you doing this?" I looked back around the room at the luminous, blue light. He reached behind the door of the bathroom and grabbed my robe. He tossed it toward me and I caught it.

"Put this on. We need to talk." He turned toward my bed, leaving me in the bathroom. I watched him take a seat on the foot of my mattress, making himself at home.

After about a minute of slow and steady breathing to calm my nerves, I wrapped and secured the robe around my body and wiggled the towel down, letting it fall to my feet. If he wanted to kill or rape me, he would have done it by now. I had decided to give him just a little bit of my trust. I needed another minute, so I paced my breath again, never taking my eyes off him and clutching my robe.

After I felt calm enough to enter my bedroom, where he was waiting for me, I moved toward the bed he was sitting on, but stopped before I reached him. I eyed the bench connected to my bay window and decided I'd feel safer over there. He chuckled as I moved as far away as I could. I took a seat, not taking my eyes off him. He, too, was watching me closely.

I looked around the room and saw more of the blue light surrounding the walls. It was so beautiful, but also terrifying.

"Who are you and what is happening?" I asked him with a trembling voice.

"I came here to protect you, Mercy. I'm sorry I scared you in the process, but I didn't know how else to just come out and tell you everything."

I looked around the room again at the blue light. I was seeing something that seemed completely impossible and beyond my understanding. I allowed my mind to open to the possibility that whatever he was about to tell me might have some truth to it.

"Why did you leave me injured after my accident? I know it was you," I said boldly, raising my brow.

"I was tracking you in my car when I saw you swerve into the forest. I know about your healing powers, so I knew you'd be okay, but you weren't healing fast enough; not how you used to. The last thing we need is for the police to become involved and ask questions. I heard someone open their door across the street, so I took off before they could see me with you. I'm so sorry. I hated seeing you hurt like that."

"I have healing powers?" I asked, now thinking about every injury that had occurred in the past week that had unnaturally disappeared within hours.

"You were born with magic that can allow your body to heal itself within minutes, sometimes seconds. When I saw you weren't healing at the accident as fast as you used to be able to, I realized you had no idea the power you held. I believe your mother was taking that power from you your entire life and shielded you from knowing who you were."

"My mother?" My pulse picked up again.

What does he know about my mom?

I closed my eyes tightly. I felt like the room was spinning now and I couldn't keep my eyes open without falling over.

I heard him speaking, but I couldn't look up.

"She was using her own magic to take away all of your powers so you could have a normal life."

"None of this is making sense to me." I looked down and touched the soft, pink flesh on my chest. "But my scar? My mom stabbed me right through the chest and it didn't heal. I have a mark to prove it."

"She must have laced it with magic. It's the only way it could have penetrated your skin the way it did without your body healing around the blade."

I removed my hand from my scar.

Hearing the words "powers" and "magic" only caused my mind to race again. I found myself staring at the wall, as if I weren't even in this conversation anymore.

My head was so out of focus, I hadn't noticed he was now standing right in front of me until I heard his voice. "Mercy, are you okay?" he asked, leaning down toward me and lifting my chin with the tip of his finger.

I finally snapped out of it and saw him looking down at me with concern in his eyes. I opened my mouth to speak, but nothing came out. I took a few deep breaths to help slow down my heartbeat and finally found the question I'd been too afraid to ask.

"What am I?"

The smile on his face was one of pride and sincerity. "You're a witch."

I blinked at him several times and leaned back, shaking my head and whispering to myself, "Of course I am." I looked up, sighing with relief.

He noticed my reaction. "You knew? Or at least, a part of you did."

"Several times growing up, I felt different. I didn't notice I was healing or a green glow shooting out of my hands. But there were times I would feel this energy in my body whenever I'd get upset, though it wasn't adrenaline. As a kid I would play make-believe that I was a witch and had these crazy powers whenever I felt them, but then the feelings would fade. I guess that was my mom's doing." I closed my eyes again, tears stinging my eyes. "I thought at times I was just crazy, or it was my imagination. When I got older, my mom told me about my ancestors, how we were descendants of some of the accused in Salem, but she told me they weren't real witches. There was a part of me that believed they were real. I tried to deny it because it scared me."

He smiled. "May I?" He gestured to the bench I was sitting on.

I didn't say yes, but I moved over a few inches, allowing him to sit. He leaned back against the bay window, keeping his eyes on me.

"I'm going to tell you a story about five children born in 1674."

I lowered my brow. "My ancestors?"

"Not exactly."

I looked at him curiously. "Okay, I'm listening."

"There were five special covens that lived in Salem from five different bloodlines, and each of them was blessed with the gift of a child. The children were each born with gifts that would help other witches with their magic."

He brought his hand to my neckline and I flinched. I realized what he was going to do and relaxed, letting him grab the jet stone necklace around my neck. He rubbed the symbol with his thumb and smiled. "You were so powerful back then."

It took me a moment to realize what he was implying.

"You're lying," I snapped.

"I have no reason to lie to you. We were born on March 2, 1674. Our mission was to train and be soldiers. The five of us were called the Chosen Ones. After we turned ten years old, we formed our *own* coven. Eight years later, we would go through what was called an Awakening. It happens when we turn eighteen on the minute we were born. An Awakening is when a witch gains all their powers to their fullest. As children, having that kind of power is dangerous, so witches aren't given all their powers at birth. Our coven decided that once we gained all of our powers, we would do another ritual right after, to make ourselves immortal, so we could live our lives protecting other witches and the humans on Earth."

"How do I not remember any of this? Do I suffer from amnesia or something?" I was now rambling, as so many questions entered my mind. "I mean, I have clear memories of myself as a kid, here in East Greenwich. Am I really that old? Does that mean my mom, Lily, and Joel have lied to me my entire life? Did they just create this story that I was born in Greenwich and—"

"No, Mercy." He stopped my questions in their tracks. "You do not understand what I'm telling you." His face looked pained as he closed his eyes. He brought his hand over to mine again and squeezed, opening his eyes again. "You died before your Awakening."

CHAPTER NINE

y eyes grew wide and my jaw dropped slightly.

"It took me centuries to find a spell to bring you back. I finally had everything I needed to reincarnate you into this life."

I couldn't find the words to speak. I was trying to wrap my mind around what he had just told me. If this was true, there was an entire life I had experienced that I knew nothing about.

Who am I?

I sat there processing all this information, my heart pounding hard against my chest.

"My father created a binding spell on the grounds of his farm. The ritual had to be done there. I met you at your home that night but the rest of the coven was still missing, so I went out to find them while you stayed back to pack a bag. You were supposed to meet us but you never showed. When we finally found you, the people in our village had already hanged you by a rope from a tree for being a witch. It was 1692 and the town was on a witch hunt. It was too late. We still had a mission and even though we were all devastated over losing you, we had to go back to the farm and complete the ritual."

I saw it. I saw *me*! I saw them in my dreams. It dawned on me that my dreams weren't dreams after all ... they were memories.

I closed my eyes and shook my head. This was overwhelming. I thought about the guy I had seen in my dreams for the past year. Was he just a dream? Or was he a memory? It wasn't Caleb, so who was he?

"After we went through our Awakening, we immediately followed it by performing an immortal spell. The villagers then found us and hanged us, too. We closed our eyes and waited until everyone left the execution, removed the nooses from our necks, and jumped down."

Wow, this is insane.

"Our coven was incomplete without you. It took me a few years to create the perfect spell to bring someone back to life in a different body. I tried several times with the witches in your bloodline, but every time they got pregnant, I couldn't use my power to bring your soul to that body. Your grandfather, thankfully, had two daughters, and at that point, I almost gave up. I then tried one last time with Daniella, and it worked. Your soul needed this body, at this time. I visited your parents and told them about the witch that was growing inside of your mother. Nine months later, she had you."

I leaned back, processing what he had been telling me. My entire life, my mom had known I was a witch.

How could she keep something like this from me?

"Mercy?" I heard Caleb say, pulling me out of my thought. "Are you still with me?"

"This is a lot to take in, Caleb," I said. "But keep going."

He leaned forward, resting his elbows on his knees. "When she was pregnant, she could feel the presence of an old soul inside of her; even your powers. She could even see visions of your past life when she laid down to sleep. I told her everything about who you were, what your mission was, and what to name you. She agreed to the terms. She was to bring you back into this world and to train you to know your magic and your heritage."

He sat up straight and shifted his body toward me. "We spoke often throughout the years. I explained to her what your powers could do and how to prepare you for your Awakening. She'd often argue with me about you being a part of this life, but I still thought she had been teaching you, Mercy. If I had known she was keeping you in the dark and taking your powers away, I would have stepped in and taken you from her. I didn't protect you. I allowed her to become addicted to your powers, which eventually led to your attack," he confessed.

It was him on the phone with my mom all these years.

"I heard you."

"You heard me?" A blank look crossed his face.

"I heard the phone calls." I shook my head and fought back tears. "I thought it was my father checking in on me, but it was you. I wondered why the calls stopped." I lowered my head.

"I'm sorry. It must hurt to realize it wasn't him," he empathized softly. My father hadn't called, he didn't care. He never cared about me.

He grabbed my hand again and rubbed the tops of my fingers. "Mercy, your powers are stronger than any witch in our coven. The level of power you were born to have is unlike anything any of us have ever seen. Your mom was never born to have that kind of power. When the Awakening happens, it will be too much for her and it will kill her."

I quickly looked up.

"You have to physically take those powers from her before you turn eighteen, or she'll die. I believe your mom wanted you dead because it was the only way for her to keep your powers. When you go through the Awakening, she won't be able to hold on to them anymore. She needs you to die for her to keep your powers. If a witch kills another witch, the surviving witch will absorb the energy and magic from the other."

"Why doesn't she just give them up now if she knows it's going to kill her? It's not like she can get to me now that she's behind locked doors."

"I don't think she realizes what will happen. Or, if she does, maybe she thinks she can get out," he said.

I didn't think that was ever a possibility, but if my mom was that powerful, maybe she would find a way.

I thought about everything he had told me. This wasn't make-believe. It was a life that was a part of me now, no matter how scary it all seemed. My ancestors were known witches. I started that car today at the park with an energy force that came through my hands and my body was healing at an unnatural speed.

"I'm a witch." I was trying to register what he was saying. "I'm an actual witch."

I thought about my mom being a witch and how she must be extremely powerful after syphoning out all my powers, on top of her own. Then there was my sweet grandfather. Wow, he had been a witch, too. That was the only way he could have passed his powers down to his children.

I was now more frightened than ever that my mom could escape and come find me. "Why hasn't she used her powers to get out of there?"

"She can't use them there. This isn't just any mental institution. This world is known for many supernatural creatures, especially in Salem. This is more of a facility to keep powers in, for those that would use their powers for evil. After she tried to kill you, one of our own used her connection to the legal system to get her transferred to her family's hospital. The walls are concealed with magic, kind of like what I did here in your room, except the powers around your room won't last. I can only hold on to them for so long. It weakens me.

"In the facility your mom is in, no one can use magic or any supernatural abilities inside the barrier. A few government officials know about us and are gladly letting us treat and control the supernatural." He grabbed my hand again. "Let me help you. You know what I am saying is true. I can take you to Salem tomorrow to see your mom and help take your powers back."

He raised his hand to my cheek, but I flinched. He was trying to be affectionate, but I didn't want him to touch me so intimately. He might know who I used to be, but I had no memory of him.

"And us?"

He smirked and chuckled under his breath. "Were we close?"

"Yeah, how close were we?" I asked.

"We were in love. Our parents knew it would be a distraction for us and our mission, so they forbade our relationship when they found out about us. We had just turned seventeen when they told us that if we didn't stop seeing each other, they would strip us of our powers."

"Did we listen?" I giggled at myself. "If I were anything back then like I am now, I wouldn't have."

He was no longer smiling. "We obeyed. It wasn't an option to disobey." He looked down and I could have sworn I saw a tear in the corner of his eye.

I hadn't really thought about my father lately, but I was now. "My father in this life, was he a witch? Or did he leave because he knew that I was?"

"Your father wasn't a witch, but I saw the fear on his face when I told them about you. Your father left out of fear, Mercy. He was a coward."

Yes, he was. Any man who walks out on his family like that is a coward. I was still so angry with what my father had done, and I didn't even remember him.

"My mom told me he had left us but would never tell me why. I assumed being a father was just too hard for him and he was running from his responsibilities." I stood up and walked away from the bench, folding my arms tight around my waist. "Do you know what happened to him?"

"I'm sorry, I don't." He stood up and walked toward me. I didn't back up.

"I believe your mom cared, loved you, and she believed taking your powers away was the best thing for you. Maybe she hoped that if she stripped you of your powers, your father would eventually come back, even just for you. Unfortunately, she couldn't stop once she started."

I huffed and shook my head, thinking about Lily now. "I can't believe Lily and Joel have been lying to me my entire life." I paused briefly. "Lily was planning to tell me something important last night, but I had my accident. This was probably it. Which means she probably knows about you and knew it was you who had been following me."

He narrowed his eyes and shook his head. "I haven't been following you, but someone has been. A few times when I tried to approach you, I heard them. I don't know who it is or what they want, but they're there. I won't let them get to you."

"You swear it wasn't you?"

He nodded. "I swear it."

"Okay, but I'm sure she knows it was you that attacked me tonight."

He sighed and shut his eyes tightly in frustration. "I didn't attack you."

"Stop, Caleb. There were better ways to handle all of this. You scared me." I moved away from him and he grabbed my wrist. I instantly yanked it away. "I don't want you to go with me tomorrow, but I will go and talk with her."

"Mercy, it's too dangerous."

"I don't trust you enough, Caleb. So, I'm going alone."

"Mercy!"

I balled my hands into fists. "Please get out of my room, Caleb, and knock down this barrier. I need to be alone right now." I stood up and pointed to the window. "I don't want you to wake Lily. Climb down the tree outside my window. I will ask Lily tomorrow how to take those powers away from my mom. I don't know how much she knows about what I can do, but I would rather have family help me than you."

He shook his head at me and let out a frustrated growl. "You're just overwhelmed by all this information. Get some rest and I will call you tomorrow." He waved his hands in the air and the blue light disappeared. He walked over to my nightstand and picked up my phone, fiddled with it, punched the keyboard a few times, and set it down.

"My number is now in your phone. Also, when you get there, you'll need to ask for Leah. She will show you how to take them. The shield prevents you from using your magic, which means you won't be able to pull the powers back into your body without the facility lowering the shield." He looked down like he was in pain. "And please, Mercy. Be careful. Your mom may not be able to use her powers on you from inside that place, but she's very manipulative. Don't trust anything she says." He walked past me, crawled through the window, and disappeared without another word.

I gasped and ran to the window. He couldn't have made that jump without getting hurt. When I peered over the window he was already running into the forest by our home, unharmed.

I ran up to my phone and opened it. He'd sent a text to himself from my phone, so he had my number.

I sat down on my bed and opened my nightstand drawer. I had

kept a knife in the drawer for protection ever since my mom attacked me. I pulled it out, closed my eyes tight, and made a small slit about an inch long. It hurt, but I had to see what would happen.

Nothing happened right away, but then after about a minute, the wound closed right before my eyes. I sat dumbfounded. This was really happening.

My phone screen told me it was almost one in the morning. I needed rest if I was going to face my mom tomorrow and make her tell me what she knew. I needed to know if everything Caleb said was the truth. If it was, maybe she would have a change of heart and willingly give me back my powers, especially if she knew it would kill her if she didn't.

CHAPTER TEN

Dressed and ready to face my mom, I stared at myself in the mirror one last time before putting my necklace back on. I was ready ... I thought.

As I entered the kitchen, Lily turned toward me, holding a warm cup of coffee and a piece of buttered toast. She smiled and took a seat at the table.

"Good morning," she said. She studied me for a minute. "Are you feeling okay? You look okay."

"I feel fine." I was suddenly nervous to bring up Caleb to her, but I had to.

I only smiled back and walked over to the pantry to grab the cereal and then to the refrigerator for the almond milk.

"Let's leave in about fifteen minutes," she instructed before taking a bite of her toast.

I grabbed my coffee and cereal and joined her at the table. We looked at each other and she stiffened up.

"You're not going to see the sketch artist today, are you?" She already knew my answer.

I shook my head. "Caleb visited me last night. He told me everything. I'm going to see my mom today."

She set her coffee down, eyes still on me.

"I was afraid of that. She told me he might come for you before your Awakening. That's what she and I talked about when she called. She wanted me to let you talk to her before he found you. I wanted to tell you, Mercy. I was going to tell you."

"You've known my whole life, Lily. And I'm guessing you knew that was him last night?" I asked.

She nodded.

"Why wait until two weeks before I'm eighteen?"

"It wasn't my place to tell you. It was your mother's. I knew Joel and I would eventually have to after your mom was arrested. A witch shouldn't do their Awakening alone. It's not like you are able to avoid it. We were just waiting for the right time to tell you."

It all sounded so comical to me.

"Is there a right time to tell me we're witches?" I asked.

"I guess not."

"Is he dangerous?" I asked her.

"I don't know. After you died, Caleb and the rest of your coven created the jet stones by enchanting them with magic, to keep the future of witches safe. They had just enough to pass down to each first-born female in each of the five bloodlines. The Chosen Ones proved to us their loyalty, but the way your mom described some of the visions of your past life, with what she saw Caleb do, she said he would only bring you destruction." She rubbed her eyes. "Is it absolutely necessary for you to go see her?"

"Caleb told me my powers are going to kill her when I go through my Awakening if I don't take them back," I explained.

Lily's mouth gaped open.

I told her what I had to do and everything Caleb had told me about myself last night. The look on her face showed me she had no idea what I was talking about. She just sat there quietly.

"This is why she tried to kill me before I turned eighteen, because she knew my powers would get too strong for her to hold on to during my Awakening. She didn't want to give them up, so killing me was the only way to assure my powers would stay inside her."

She looked panicked. "The visions your mom had of your life were terrifying to her. She'd cry day and night every time she caught a glimpse of your previous life. There were days when she was pregnant with you when she would just close her eyes, but she wasn't sleeping. Visions flashed in her mind constantly. She said you were always on the run, fighting evil beings that threatened the witches in your village. Your magic was so dark, she feared bringing you into this world. Caleb and his family used dark magic and you were always with him. She was afraid you would use that type of magic in this life. She told me she was going to find a way to take your powers away so you could live a normal, innocent life. I didn't know what your powers would do to her, or that they would cause her to hurt her own daughter."

"I don't have a choice here, Lily. Either way, my Awakening will bring my powers back into my body, but I don't want them to kill my mom in the process. I have to take them back or ask her to give them up."

"Would you like me to come with you?" she asked.

I shook my head. "No. That hospital barrier will protect me, right?"

She nodded. "Then I need to go alone."

"Please call me when you're heading back."

It was nice not to have to argue with her like I had with Caleb.

I grabbed my purse and turned back to Lily. "Do you use your powers?"

"No." She shook her head. "I wanted a normal life for myself. Besides, my powers don't even come close to the amount of strength inside you." She walked up to me and placed her hand on mine.

I welcomed her touch with a small squeeze.

"You're special, Mercy. Joel and I will be here to help you in any way we can."

I flashed her a smile and released her hand. "I'll be back by six."

I arrived at the hospital ninety minutes later and checked in at the front desk. I glanced down the hall and noticed steel bars on windows of each room. One of the guards standing near the front desk had a long pipe device attached to his belt. It looked like a stun gun, but longer and thinner.

Could this be a magic device to control whatever creatures lie behind these steel doors?

"I'm Mercy Brawling," I told the red-haired, chubby woman at the front desk. I handed her my driver's license and she glanced at me once.

"Hold out your wrist," she said expressionless. I held out my right hand and she placed a hospital band around my wrist with my name on it, the date, the time, and my mother's name. "Mr. Kriser will escort you to the visiting room. No touching. Got it?"

"Got it." I looked around and didn't see anyone else. "I'm supposed to meet someone named Leah."

The woman looked back up. "She's on her way. You're a little early." She signaled to the guard next to me.

The same guard with the pipe device, whose name tag read George Kriser, opened the door for me and led me down a long hallway that took us to a large lounge area. I first noticed how simple the room was. There were a few televisions, a long sectional, and several tables lining the walls. We passed by an empty admin desk and turned the corner heading toward a table at the center of the room. I saw my mom sitting quietly with her arms folded, staring right at me as I approached.

My stomach churned, and I could feel my heart pounding violently against my chest. She looked tired, worn, and sick. Were they not taking care of her here? She may have tried to kill me, but she was still a human being, and she was still my mom.

I'll have Lily call her lawyers tomorrow to make sure she's being treated right.

"Daniella, your daughter is here to see you."

He looked at me and gestured toward the table where she sat. "Sit here. No touching. And if at any point you want to leave, just throw your hand up and I'll take you back. I'll be right over there." George pointed to the doorway and then walked away. I watched him take a position in the doorway, fold his arms, and stand in a wide stance.

"So, Lily agreed to our terms. I knew she would." My mother spoke before I took a seat. The smug look on her face was unsettling.

I pulled my chair out and sat down at the table across from her. "I need to talk to you." My arms were folded stubbornly.

"Since I called you here, I think I have the right to speak first. We don't want things to get ugly again, do we?"

Her threat terrified me, but I kept my breathing calm and steady. I knew I was protected by these walls and George over in the corner had a wicked little device I was sure could do some damage if she were to go all psycho on me again.

"I didn't come here because you summoned me. I need answers."

Her eyes were heavy and the dark circles under her eyes showed me she didn't sleep much. She looked like she'd aged twenty years since she had been admitted.

"Caleb found me and told me everything. I know why you did what you did," I said.

She giggled, throwing her head back. "Oh darling, if you knew everything, then you wouldn't be here this close to me." Her smile disappeared and her expression made my skin crawl.

I looked over at George, contemplating if this were a good idea. Maybe I should have brought Caleb after all. And where was Leah?

My mom knew what to say to make the fear come back. I cleared my throat and tapped my foot against the floor nervously.

"I need more answers than what he's telling me and I think you know. Lily mentioned you had visions of me while you were pregnant. Is that true?"

"Yes. I saw you do harrowing things with the magic you were born with. I was protecting you in this life. You should be thanking me." She lowered her head and stared at her hands that were clutched together. "I did what I had to do."

I couldn't hold back the tears any longer. My heart ached at what she'd become. What happened to the funny and loving mom that I once knew?

"Why are you doing this? Do my powers affect you that much, that the love you had for your own daughter has completely disappeared?"

She stared right through me and then closed her eyes. I looked down at her hands and they were clenched in fists. She opened her eyes. "You haven't tasted the pleasure of your powers, Mercy. You haven't felt the energy flow through you like I have. You may be feeling a little bit here and a little bit there, but not like this. I felt your powers trying to leave my body a week before your graduation and I couldn't give them up. I can't give them up. I am nothing without them."

She relaxed her fists and for a moment, she looked like she was going to pass out. She held her head and swayed slightly side to side.

She is insane. Do I really want this kind of power? Would I become like this?

"Why did you ask Lily to have me come?" I asked.

"Because I know I'm going to lose your powers in a few weeks. I can barely hold on to them now. I was hoping you'd see how dangerous they really are for you and give them to me. There's a way to lower the shield in this place that will allow you to transfer them to me. If you just do that, I'll spare your life." She giggled again, while her body shook slightly.

She has completely lost her mind.

"Mercy?" a woman interrupted from behind me. My mom stopped laughing.

"My name is Leah. Will you walk with me?"

Leah had straight, shoulder length brown hair and blue eyes. She wore a black business blazer over a red blouse and a black pencil skirt with tall black heels. She was also extremely petite, and if it weren't for her heels, I would guess she was about five feet.

She looked familiar but I couldn't recall from where. "Do I know you?

"My family owns this institution."

No, that's not it.

She placed her hand on my shoulder. "Please." She gestured toward the hallway.

I looked at my mom who wore that same smug smile, though her hands were shaking. "Yes, of course." I stood and walked with her to the hallway next to the recreational room.

"I just got off the phone with Caleb. He's waiting in the parking lot for you."

"He followed me here?" My blood was now boiling.

She ignored my question. "We don't have much time. In a moment, you are going to go back into that room. When I give the signal, you'll grab your mother's hands and take your powers back. The only way this can be done is if we lower the shield in the room.

We can't lower the entire shield in the hospital, for safety reasons, of course. Wear this." She handed me a black bracelet. "This bracelet is enchanted. If you wear it when you touch her, you'll be able to draw your powers out of her and back into you."

My eyes were drawn to her wrist and I noticed she was wearing one, too. Was she also a witch?

"But be cautious, Mercy," she warned. "When she realizes the barrier is down, she will try to use her magic to stop you. Because she also has your magic inside of her, she'll be stronger than all of us here."

Her warning made my stomach twist into knots. But I also wondered if I should trust her. She, just like Caleb, was a stranger to me. She also associated with Caleb, who alone made me nervous every time he simply stared at me.

"I'm scared, Leah," I confessed.

She smiled. "You're the strongest witch I know. You don't remember, but we were like sisters." She placed her hand on my shoulder and I instantly felt a bond and connection to her. It was warm and loving. She wasn't just any witch from my past, she was part of my coven.

She leaned over and peered into the room where my mother sat and looked back at me. "Put on the bracelet."

I did as she asked and we both peered inside the room. "Let's go," she instructed, gesturing to the door.

We were now heading back into the recreational room where my mom was still sitting patiently. Leah was behind me with her arms folded. I sat down and stared into my mother's dark eyes. The only sound was the ticking of the clock on the wall.

I then heard a whisper from Leah's lips.

"Now," she whispered gently.

CHAPTER ELEVEN

I reached out my hands and grabbed my mom's wrists. She immediately resisted, as if she knew what was happening. My hands felt like they were on fire. She tried hard to pull her hands away, but I was surprisingly stronger. The windows in the room shattered and my mom's eyes grew darker and darker until they were as black as the night she tried to take my life.

"Let me go, Mercy. You don't know what you're doing!" She twisted her wrists from my grip, then wrapped her fingers around my own hands and squeezed against them until I felt every bone in my hands snap into pieces.

I screamed from the pain. Suddenly Leah was by my side, but she didn't intervene.

"Leah, make her stop! Help me!" my mother pleaded.

My hands were useless, but my powers were already coming back to me and I was able to fight her. My mom closed her eyes tightly, as if she were battling the worst migraine of her life.

"Stop! Stop!" she screamed. I watched as my mom grew weaker.

I felt an overwhelming amount of power consume me while the power drained from my mom and into me. The bones in my hands repaired themselves instantly and then I felt my mom's own powers consume me. I was absorbing her magic as well. I could feel the power shifting from my mom's hands into mine, moving up my arms and filling my entire body. The feeling was unlike anything I had ever felt before. It was powerful and intoxicating.

Then everything stopped as my mom fell to the ground.

"Mom!" I looked at Leah. "What happened? Leah, what is happening to her?"

Leah looked concerned, but not surprised. I tried to move my mom, but she was lifeless. I couldn't control the sobs that overwhelmed me. The pain I felt, both physically and emotionally, was excruciating.

I looked back up at Leah. "Is she dead?" She didn't say anything, but a look of shame spread across her face. She had known this would happen.

I shook my mom. "Mom. Wake up! Wake up!" I shook her again, but she was completely limp. I checked her pulse and I couldn't feel a beat.

"What did I do? I thought if I took them, she would be okay."

Leah knelt to the floor, hesitated for a moment, and gently placed her hand on my back.

"Your mother had a brain tumor, Mercy. It was going to kill her, anyway. Your powers were the only thing keeping her alive the past four years. She was going to die now, or in a week when you go through your Awakening." She removed her hand from my back and stood up. "I'm sorry I didn't tell you, but you would have hesitated or chosen not to do this altogether. It would have been so much more painful for her, during your transition. You showed her mercy."

My heart ripped into a million pieces. "I trusted you guys."

The pain my mom went through was my fault. I did this. I knew what she had done to me was so much worse, but seeing her dead now, in my arms, was more than I could handle. I wanted to take it back. Take everything back. Tears didn't stop for what felt like hours, as I clung to my mom's lifeless body.

Lily and I didn't want to prolong my mother's cremation, so the next afternoon, we made all the arrangements. We decided against a memorial service, as she had no friends in our community anymore. They all knew what she had done. Everyone who knew her had feared her, and everyone who didn't only knew her as what they had read in the papers: a monster who tried to kill her only daughter.

Joel flew in the following night, and Thursday, we spread her ashes over Salem Harbor, where my grandfather had met my nana. Joel was filled in on the details of the past few weeks and he and Lily helped me learn to harness my powers as much as they could. Joel was a practicing witch, but he had completely different powers than I did. Lily hadn't used her powers since she was fourteen. Even when she went through her Awakening at eighteen, she didn't use them. We both saw Lily's excitement in using her powers for the first time in years. She had missed it.

"So, you can also turn a car on with your hands?" I asked, remembering the first time I saw what my magic could do.

"I may or may not have stolen my dad's car a few times as a kid," she confessed.

Joel and I both shook our heads and laughed at her. Joel stood up and walked over to the center of the family room. He put his hands up. "This spell usually takes every ounce of energy I have, but it's my favorite. A vortex is so complex. The slightest inconsistency or error can collapse the entire thing. William showed me how to do this when I was five."

He moved his hands around left to right, right to left, as yellow energy grew brighter and brighter, until it formed a large vertical ring.

"Wow," I gasped. "That's insane but beautiful."

I walked up to it and placed my hand on the outer ring, my fingers lingering near the black hole at the center. I moved my hand forward and it went inside. I quickly retracted it back up against my body. "Whoa!"

The portal shut down in front of me. "Another day, Mercy."

Man, the things I missed out on growing up. This is unreal.

By that next Friday, I was exhausted beyond belief. I had just woken up from a restless night again, filled with haunting images of what I now understood to be memories. Opening only one eye, I noticed the time was eight. I showered and ran out the door with plans to meet Shannon at Krista's donut shop for coffee and pastries.

As I walked toward my car, I saw Caleb leaning against the bumper. My heart leaped out of my chest. Half because that man was incredibly gorgeous, but half because it startled me to see him. After I had left the psychiatric ward, I wouldn't look at him. He knew, just as Leah had known, what that would do to my mom, and I couldn't feel anything but betrayal toward them.

He was staring at me with his beautiful eyes as I cautiously approached him.

"What are you doing here?" I snapped.

"I just wanted to say, in person, how sorry I am about your mom, but I *am* glad it was her and not you. You have your powers now and she can't ever hurt you again."

"You have no right to speak to me about my mother!" I shouted.

"Whoa, Mercy. Nothing I have done was to hurt you. Sorry if you don't agree with the way we handled it, but if she had hurt you, or worse, killed you, I would never have forgiven myself. I'm sorry you had to watch her die like that."

"Damn you, Caleb. Stay away from me today. I'm not in the mood."

"Here." He reached toward me and I slapped his hand away, backing up a few steps.

"Don't you dare touch me!" I warned.

Caleb laughed as if I were amusing him. He was so annoyingly arrogant.

"You forgot to put this on today." He dangled my jet stone necklace by one finger.

My eyes widened, and my hand flew to my chest.

"Were you in my room just now?"

"I told you. I'm here to protect you. It's foolish for you to not wear this now. Put it on."

He is so demanding. What right does he have to order me around?

I snatched it from his hand. "I don't need, nor want, your protection. I have enough power now that I can take care of myself. Plus, I have Lily and Joel to help me."

"Wear it, Mercy. You're not immortal ... yet."

I gave him a dirty look and grabbed the necklace. "Stay away from me today and stay out of my room." I pulled the chain around my neck and tried to fasten it.

"Stupid chain." I couldn't get it to latch.

"Do you mind?" he asked with a smirk as he took a step forward. I backed up.

"I've got it," I snapped, trying to latch it again.

He sighed and was already tracing my neckline delicately with his fingers. I froze. His touch sent goosebumps over my skin and I had to control my breathing. I had never had a guy affect me like this.

He fastened the necklace and stepped back.

"Thanks," I said. I was embarrassed at how weak I acted around him.

I fiddled with my keys and unlocked the truck. "I have to go. I'm meeting my friend."

Caleb glared at me again. His eerie stares were making me uncomfortable, as if he were analyzing every part of my face. He slowly approached me and placed his hands on my shoulders gently. He traced his fingers up my neck. I wanted to push him away, but for some reason, I paused. Then he pulled me in and planted his lips on mine. For a moment, I let him kiss me, but I stopped him when I realized this was not okay. None of this was okay.

I placed my hands on his chest, feeling a surge of energy and strength radiating through my arms. I didn't ask for what happened next, but it just happened on its own. That same green ray of energy from the other night in the truck blasted him across the driveway through my fingertips.

Holy shit.

"Caleb! I'm so sorry."

I had just meant to push him away. I had no idea I could even do that. I then snapped out of my pity for him as he laughed, still lying on his back.

"What the hell, Caleb?"

He slowly clamored back on his feet. "That's some power you've got there, Mercy."

This jerk was laughing at me. "Who do you think you are? I'm not some high school skank that will let any cocky guy kiss me anytime he wants."

He was still laughing.

Unbelievable!

"I never said you were, but it got you to use your powers without any help from Lily or any worthless spell." He grinned while brushing off the gravel from his arm and stood up.

That was all a trick just to piss me off to use my powers.

"I'm leaving." I quickly climbed into the truck.

Caleb smiled again then said, "See you soon."

He climbed into his own vehicle and drove off before me. I couldn't hold back my tears any longer.

I hate him! I hate him!

I repeated this again and again in my mind as I sobbed uncontrollably.

CHAPTER TWELVE

After breakfast with Shannon, we hung out at her place for a few hours. I only shared with her my emotions over my mom's death, being careful to not mention Caleb. I knew it would lead to too many questions that could then lead to me having to explain that I was a witch, and she wasn't ready for that.

Shannon and I worked on some music all Friday afternoon with my guitar and her perfect set of vocal cords. I hadn't picked up my guitar since right before graduation. I had left a message for Cami to let her know about my mom earlier in the week, but she had never replied. It was odd for her to not be there for me when I needed her. None of us had heard from her, but when we reached out to Cami's mom, she told us she had seen her come and go, so we knew she was at least safe.

Once it was five in the evening, we walked into Mario's Pizza and Shannon headed to the line. I looked over and saw Cami four rows behind us, sitting with Larry Bridges from our high school football team.

"What's up with Cami and Larry?" I asked Shannon as she joined me at the table with our pizzas. "Did you ever end up hearing from her this week? She hasn't returned my calls and now she's on a date with Larry." I looked to Shannon quizzically. "Maybe she didn't get the message?"

Shannon frowned. "No, she got the message. Something is up with her. I mean, when has she *ever* shown interest in Larry Bridges? Never. That's when."

"That's not like Cami. I wonder what's going on." I knew we girls had a bad week from time to time, but we never let anything bother us to the point of being rude to our friends for no reason. She hadn't even responded to my voicemail about my mother dying. There was no "sorry for your loss" or "I'm a shoulder to cry on."

Thirty minutes later, Riley finally joined us.

"So, who's the new hot guy with Jessica? He's so cute." Shannon's voice pulled Riley and me out of our side conversation.

I looked behind me, confused, and saw Jessica with the one person I didn't expect to see her with—Caleb.

Jessica was by far the loudest person at our school. You could hear her telling someone a secret from a hundred lockers away. Jessica was shouting a joke in Caleb's ear and it was obvious he was trying to get my attention by his fake laughter.

Jessica had been in my biology class this past year and I had talked with her a few times at parties over the summer. She looked stunning, but her features were gigantic. Even her eyes were huge, like a cartoon character. She had long brown hair, and unnaturally bright blue eyes, which we all assumed were colored contacts.

Shannon tilted her head to check out his butt as he bent down to pick up Jessica's purse, which she had probably dropped on purpose.

"I've never seen him before," I lied.

Caleb turned around in our direction as soon as I had said that. "Hey, Mercy. Funny running into you like this," Caleb said, now standing by our booth. I didn't look up. I'm not going to play this game. "I'm Caleb." He reached out his hand and greeted both Shannon and Riley.

"So, Caleb, how did you and Mercy meet?" Shannon asked.

"We met a long time ago, actually. I came back into town and we ran into each other on Main," he lied for the both of us.

I sighed with relief.

I finally looked up. "How did you meet Jessica? You didn't go to our school."

What I really wanted to ask him was what kind of game he was playing.

"After you so rudely drove off after I brought you back your necklace, she was on the side of the road, trying to change a tire all by herself. I helped her and she wanted to repay me by buying me dinner." He flashed a huge grin and Jessica's cheeks turned red.

He continued. "Jennifer has been the only person in town to show me hospitality."

"Jessica," Jessica mumbled under her breath. Shannon laughed out loud, nearly choking on her bite of pizza.

"Are you done now?" I snapped. He was really pissing me off.

"Why are you acting like you care so much what I do?" he asked.

"I don't. You're just incredibly annoying." I turned my back to him.

I thought about that. Why *did* I care so much what he said or did? I didn't want him. He was arrogant and dangerous. Yes, I was attracted to him and we had some relationship history, but none of that mattered. He manipulated me into taking my powers from my mom, without telling me what would happen. He forced a kiss on me, just so that I would use my magic. I couldn't trust him.

He turned to Jessica and tucked a stray hair behind her ear. She turned red again.

"Jessica, are you ready to go?"

"Ready when you are." She perked up and glanced around at us, hoping to see that we cared. No one looked up. No one cared.

He looked back at me and winked as they walked out the door.

"Can anyone be more annoying?" I complained once they left.

"I thought he was charming," Shannon admitted, tilting her head as he walked away, checking out his butt again.

Riley huffed. "I didn't."

Of course he didn't.

I looked out the restaurant window and saw Caleb and Jessica getting into his car.

Where is he taking her and why do I care so much? Ugh, I care. And I hate myself for it.

As everyone talked during dinner, I tried not to think about him. *Tried* being the key word. It just wasn't possible. I kept picturing Caleb with Jessica and wondering if they were still hanging out. Did he want to date her? Was he just trying to make me jealous?

We had been at Mario's for over an hour and it was getting dark. I needed a distraction. "We should have a bonfire tonight," I suggested to Riley and Shannon.

"That sounds like a great idea." Shannon was already whipping out her cell phone and sending out mass text messages to everyone she knew. And she knew everyone.

Just then, Cami barged over to us, practically pushing people over on her way.

She stopped inches away, glaring at me. "Look at you, Miss Perfect. Now you have two guys who want you. How are you going to play this game with them?" she snapped.

I stood up and put my hands up, putting distance between us. "Cami, what are you talking about?" I asked.

"You've broken up with Riley and yet you still torture him by constantly being in his life. Then, this new guy comes around who clearly is using Jessica to get to you. Well, aren't you lucky." She looked around at the restaurant. Everyone was staring, and it only fueled her. "Look everyone, Mercy Brawling, the tease."

This isn't Cami. This can't be the girl I've known for the last four years.

"Cami, you can't be serious right now. How long have we been friends? Are you even hearing the words coming out of your mouth right now?" I asked.

"You're messing with his head. Riley deserves better," she snarled.

"I know he does," I admitted, while holding back the tears I knew were about to come.

Everyone looked uncomfortable with her outburst, especially Riley. Cami started to say something else, but Shannon jumped between us.

"Shut up, Cami. A little insensitive, don't you think? Her mom just died and you couldn't even call her back. What the hell is wrong with you? Daniella was like a mother to you!" Shannon was now inches from Cami's face.

Cami looked at me and then back at Shannon. She had tears in her eyes, but her face remained hard. She was fighting the tears and trying to stay mad, but I could tell she hated what was coming out of her mouth.

I stepped closer to Cami and whispered. "Stop, Cami. This isn't you." I spoke softly and placed my hand on her shoulder. She flinched and poked me hard against the chest with her forefinger.

"Watch your back," she warned. She then walked out the door, leaving us and her date.

My jaw dropped. She had never acted like this before toward me, or to anyone. What was wrong with her?

"Thanks a lot, Riley," I snapped at him.

"What was I supposed to say, Mercy? Anything that came out of my mouth would have just pissed her off more."

I shook my head, realizing he was right.

Once everyone calmed down, we agreed we needed to get to the bonfire while we still had light so we could get it all set up. We also needed that distraction, now.

We arrived at the cliffs in Newport slightly after seven thirty. The firewood and drinks were already taken care of, so Riley and I rushed over to help build the fire. I was now scanning the incoming crowd for Cami. I wanted her to show up, so we could talk about what had happened at the diner. I refused to lose one of my best friends over literally nothing.

Caleb pulled up in his black shiny car an hour after we arrived. He emerged from his vehicle as I approached.

"No Jessica?" I asked.

"You know that's not who I want."

I gulped. Butterflies fluttered around in my stomach. How could I hate him so much, but also get excited when he says stuff like that?

He scanned the crowd at the beach. "I need to find Cami." Of course, that stung. Had I read this all wrong?

"I'm trying to find her, too. But please, Caleb. Leave her alone. She's going through something and—"

"I have to find her. Don't go anywhere." He turned and headed toward the cliff along the shore line.

Of course he wasn't going to listen to me. What did he want from her? He had shown no interest in her so far, so this had to be part of his stupid mind games.

I then felt a hand on mine.

"Sorry." Riley quickly apologized and retracted his hand.

"No, it's okay. I've actually been fine lately with contact."

It was weird. Touch was no longer bothering me, except when Caleb kissed me, but that was for a completely different reason. I wondered if it had to do with my healing powers that were stronger than ever now.

"Well, that's good." He smiled at me. "You up for a walk?"

"Caleb told me to wait ... oh forget it, let's go."

I zipped up my hoodie. We linked arms and headed toward the beach.

We walked along the water and didn't say anything at first, but then I decided this silence thing wasn't working for me.

"Hey, Riley?"

"What's up?"

"This isn't going to be weird, is it? Between you and me?"

"No. Not unless you make it weird." He smiled and I relaxed. "We're too close."

I wasn't sure if my next question was going to make things awkward, but I still needed to ask. "What Cami said at Mario's, is that how you feel? Does it bother you that I still call you and need you in my life?"

He shook his head and smiled. "Are you kidding me, Mercy? You're my best friend. Being in your life is the only thing that helps me get up in the morning. And I don't mean that to put pressure on you or make you feel obligated. What Cami said about it torturing me? That's a lie."

I let out a deep sigh of relief. I knew what Cami said was irrational, but her words made me think about what my actions were really doing to the people around me.

I looked up at my best friend and knew I could trust him more than anyone and I needed someone to talk to. I had to tell someone about what was going on with me.

"I need to tell you something. Something only a few people know."

"You can tell me anything."

We stopped walking and sat on wooden rickety stairs that led to the sand from a beach parking lot.

No reason to beat around the bush.

I bent down and moved the sand around, grabbing a seashell that had a small chipped piece on one side of it. I took the sharp part from the chip and placed it on my skin, dragging it slowly to leave a small cut in the center of my palm.

"What are you doing? Mercy, stop."

"Wait," I said.

After a few seconds, the wound healed.

His eyes widened. "Whoa. How?"

"I'm a witch and one of my powers is the power to heal." I waited for a response but he just stared at me. "Witches are real. Like, not just stories in books or movies, but, like … real. The Salem witch hunt happened to real witches."

"Are you messing with me?" He half smiled, but when he noticed I wasn't smiling, he dropped his grin and lowered his brow. He looked back at my palm. "That's not a trick you're doing there?"

I shook my head. "It all started in 1674." I then told him the short version of everything, from me being born centuries ago, to Caleb and our connection, to what really happened to my mother and why she had tried to kill me.

He looked like he had seen a ghost and wouldn't say a word. So, I kept talking.

"You know," I continued. "I've always felt like there was more than this, more than what we could comprehend. My mom and dad moved to East Greenwich a few years before I was born. All my ancestors are from Salem. I'm from the same bloodline as my original body."

"You're a witch." He said. It wasn't a question. He believed me. He knew I wouldn't lie to him, even with something this weird and unbelievable. Also, the wound healing the way it did couldn't be unseen. That happened. It was real.

"Everything Caleb has told me has been true so far, but I don't know if I can trust him completely. He didn't even tell me that my mom was going to die once I took my powers back. I felt completely betrayed."

"What has Lily said about him? You said she knew about your life before this. She must know something about him."

"She wasn't sure. She said my mom saw us together in her visions, and saw me do terrible things with him."

"Then you need to stay away from him." He grabbed my hand gently.

"I wish it were that easy. He won't leave me alone and I've seen what his magic can do."

I went to speak again when we heard several high-pitched screams echo from the direction of the bonfire.

We both jumped up and ran back to the fire as fast as we could. When we approached the bonfire, I saw Cami lying on a blanket, covered in blood.

Oh my God. Oh my God.

Peter from my school was pacing back and forth with Cami's blood on his hands.

He stopped pacing and turned to me. "We heard a scream and saw Cami falling over the cliff. It took all five of us to get her back up the trail. She's alive, but she isn't responding to us. She must have slipped. We were going to leave her in case her neck or something was broken, but the current was starting to flood over her. She would have drowned." His voice was trembling.

"I am on the phone with 911 now. They're close," I heard a female voice say, but I didn't look to see who it was.

I looked down at Cami. Through the pool of blood covering her body, I could still see her chest rising. She was alive.

She opened her eyes as I walked closer to her. Once I was a few inches from her, she looked up at me and grabbed my arm firmly. "He's trying to kill you." Her voice was soft and weak.

My eyes widened as I looked around the crowd. Everyone looked at each other, trying to figure out what she had just said.

"Cami, what are you talking about? Who's trying to kill me?" I asked her quietly, so only she could hear.

"He's coming for you."

"Who?"

Her eyes slowly closed.

No, no, no! Cami, wake up!

Panic was rising in my chest. I couldn't control the sobs that were forcing their way to the surface. "Cami, wake up!" I shook her shoulders. "Wake up!" I put my fingers on her wrist and felt a pulse.

There's a pulse!

I looked up just as the paramedics arrived. I stepped back to give them space and backed up into Caleb.

I turned around and shoved him back. Several people looked our way, but I calmed myself down long enough for them to lose interest and look back at Cami.

"I had nothing to do with this," he said calmly, so as not to draw any more attention.

"You went to find her and then this happened. Come to think of it, everything crazy that has happened in the last few weeks has happened since you came into town. What do you expect me to think?"

"I expect you to trust me." He gritted his teeth.

"You make it really damn hard." I took a deep breath and wiped the tears from my eyes with the sleeve of my shirt. I looked back over toward Cami and saw that the paramedics were taking her away.

Caleb wrapped his arms around my waist from behind, pulling my back into his chest. I froze but didn't pull away. He lowered his head toward my ear.

"She's under a spell, Mercy. She'd been possessed. There's nothing we can do but find the witch who did this to her."

I turned around, facing him and he released his grasp. "Another witch did this?"

He nodded.

I was frozen, realizing what this meant. They weren't just stalking me, they were hurting the ones I love to get to me.

"I will find out who did this, and I won't stop until they're dead," I warned, my voice steady and firm like the ground beneath my feet.

My own words scared me. Was I willing to kill someone to protect the ones I love? In that moment, there was no doubt in my mind I would.

CHAPTER THIRTEEN

The scene at the hospital was a nightmare. Everyone was crying and Cami's mom, Laurie, was barely functioning while waiting for updates about her daughter. She had been drowning herself in the vodka she always kept disguised inside her water bottle. She only fooled the ones who didn't know her.

The doctors had told us Cami was in a coma and they weren't sure when she'd wake up. But we knew she had been put under a spell. The only ones who knew the truth were the ones who knew our secrets.

Caleb and I were back in my room and he waited for me to shower and get ready for bed. I sat next to him on my mattress, curling my feet under my legs to get comfortable.

For the next hour, we tried to make sense of what had happened. Caleb was convinced that she had been possessed for several days now, which would explain her aggressive behavior toward me, and the fact that she hadn't returned my call after hearing of my mom's death. He felt dark energy surrounding her that he was able to detect after years of being around the supernatural.

Caleb suggested that whoever did this was doing it to get to me. They were trying to use Cami to hurt me, to destroy me. But who? And why? Aside from my mom, who would hate me enough to want me dead?

"So that wasn't you I saw watching me from the window? You haven't been following me before the day you approached me at the park?" I asked.

He shook his head, and the unsettling feeling of being watched again twisted in my stomach.

"What kind of person was I back then?" I asked.

Caleb looked down and fiddled with his ring, which bore his family crest. After a long pause, he looked up and brushed my hair behind my ear. He was holding back again. He wanted to tell me something, but he couldn't. Or wouldn't. Again, what was he hiding?

"What happened to Cami could have happened to you. This is why I fight so hard to help you with your powers. If you don't know how to defend yourself against the supernatural, you'll lose."

"I didn't ask for this," I said sharply.

"Neither did I." Caleb looked over at my window and sighed. "I have a few leads I'm going to follow up on." He tilted my chin up so I was looking at him. "I love you, Mercy." He leaned in and kissed my forehead. "I'll call you once I know more. Don't do anything reckless. Stay close to Lily. She'll protect you until I return."

He loves me?

My mind drifted off after I heard him say those three little words. Did he really love me? He may have loved the Mercy in the seventeenth century, but I'm not that person anymore. And years had passed. He didn't even know the real me. Did he?

"I was serious when I said you were special. There are enemies out there that fear you and will use everything they can to come after you. They know you have your powers again and they know you are about to go through an Awakening. Please let me train you."

"I know I need to train. Give me a few days and I'll be ready."

He looked down and closed his eyes tightly, as if he were in pain, and then looked back up. "Sorry I kissed you. I was trying to force you to use your powers the way you used to, by instinct; usually driven by fear or anger."

I placed my hand on his cheek. "You could have just asked me, Caleb."

"You act like you hate me."

"Well, then, stop being so arrogant." I gave him a slight smile, and stepped in his direction, closing the gap between us. "You will know when I want you to kiss me." He brushed my hair away from my face again. "Things are going to be very different tomorrow, Caleb. I am still mourning my mother's death and now Cami is under a spell she can't wake up from. These next two days alone will be good for me. Let me know what you find out."

He nodded.

"Caleb?" He stopped just before he got to the door and turned around. "What powers do you have, aside from creating sound proof auras around a room?"

"I can control fire." He opened his palm and flames instantly radiated from his hand. I looked at his face and his eyes looked more amber and vibrant.

The flame disappeared, and he grabbed my hand. He turned my hand over, palm facing up. He turned his hands over and held them next to mine. The lines on our palms were identical. My heart pounded in my chest.

How is that possible?

"The Chosen Ones may be from different families, but we're all connected. We all have different powers, but our most prominent one is the element we represent. I represent Fire, so I can control it." He closed his hand.

"Ah, yes. Your tattoo," I said. "And Leah? I felt a connection with her. She was part of the coven."

He smiled. "She can control Water."

He held up his hand outward now, pointing his fingers up.

"We each came from a different bloodline but formed our own coven. Each of us represents an element that other witches harness their powers from."

"Lily told me about the elements when explaining the pentagram to me, but not this detailed."

He pointed at his thumb. "You are different than the rest of us. I control Fire. Leah is Water." He skipped over the middle finger. "Ezra represents Earth and Simon represents Air." He dropped his hand.

"I'm the middle finger?" I snickered. "How am I so different?"

Anxiety filled my body, waiting for the answer he had so far withheld from me—the answer to who I was.

"Though your bloodline represents the element of Spirit, you Mercy, can control all the elements at once. None of us are able to do that."

"I control *all* the elements? Why? What does that even mean?" I asked.

"You were the leader of our coven. You were brought here to bring balance. By you getting your powers back and going through your Awakening, you will restore the balance that has been lost for centuries. Without Spirit and without the power to bring all five elements together, we can't win this fight."

"What's going to happen to me on my eighteenth birthday?" This was the question I really feared, but I needed to know before it happened. I needed to be prepared.

"You'll go through your Awakening. The moment the hour strikes at the time you were born, you will feel all your powers come to you, stronger than they were when you took them from your mom. The only difference between your Awakening and other witches, is that I need to draw blood from you to bind you to the coven when it happens. It won't hurt, though. Also ..."

"Also?"

"You'll perform the immortal spell like the rest of our coven did. I can perform the ritual myself, and—"

"No."

His hands balled into fists. "You have to," he argued like a stubborn child.

"No, I don't."

I'd thought about this a lot since he had told me what they had done. I knew this was coming, and I wasn't going to be a part of that.

He huffed and shook his head. "You understand why it's so important, right?"

"Yes, I know. You don't want to lose me again."

I did get it. I knew why he wanted this, and a part of me agreed with him. My coven needed me, and they couldn't risk losing me again, but being immortal and living forever, I wasn't so sure I could do that. I couldn't watch every single person I loved die while I continued to live.

He placed his hands on my cheeks, caressing them gently. His eyes seemed to pierce right through to my soul, drawing me in; however, I knew I had all the power. I slowly put my hands on each side of his face.

"Caleb?"

"Yes?"

"I want you to kiss—"

His lips were on mine before I could finish my sentence. The kiss was fierce, but gentle. He delicately grabbed the back of my neck and kissed me deeper. Goose pimples covered my skin as he gently caressed my neckline.

Suddenly, flashes entered my mind while we kissed. I saw his face, but we weren't here in my room. We were in the middle of a small village and Caleb was holding a wooden weapon in his hand while sharpening the edges. The images were as clear as if I were there. I could smell the haystacks against a barn next to us and the fire pit burning behind me.

I snapped back to the present and quickly pulled myself from our embrace. "Caleb, I just saw something," I said, excitement rising in my voice.

"When we kissed?" He looked surprised.

"Kiss me again." I grabbed the back of his neck and brought him in for another kiss.

My mind traveled back to the village. I recognized one of the old buildings from Salem but there were many shops that should have been there but weren't. Suddenly, I realized what I was seeing. This was a memory from my previous life.

"Behind you!" Caleb tossed me the weapon he had been sharpening. I turned around and plunged it into a man's chest.

The vision disappeared again, and I pushed Caleb off me. "What was that?"

"Mercy, relax. It's okay." He tried to pull me in, but I pushed him away again.

"What did I do? I just watched myself kill a man!" I was now in full panic mode.

He was breathing heavily. "Relax, please. I can explain."

"Get away from me. You helped me kill someone. Oh my God, Caleb." I turned and ran toward the door, but he pressed his hand against it so I couldn't pull it open.

"It's okay, Mercy. You're not a murderer. What you saw yourself killing wasn't human."

"Get out!" I could hear Lily running down the hallway. She burst in the room.

"Mercy, are you okay?" she asked, panic in her voice.

I nodded.

She looked over at Caleb. "You need to go. Now." I had never seen Lily this upset before. She moved to stand between us and turned back to face Caleb. "I said get out!"

He held up his hands in defeat. "All right." He turned back to me. "I'll call you tomorrow."

As he walked out my bedroom, he scowled at Lily.

She hugged me tightly after we heard the door slam shut downstairs. She quickly ran through the house shutting every window and locking them.

Lily went back into her room after she was confident the house was as secure as she could make it, not that it would stop Caleb from using his magic to get inside. I didn't tell her about my visions because that would only make her more nervous, and I needed her calm.

After Lily finally left me alone in my room, I laid back down on my pillow, trying to get to sleep. I tossed and turned for several hours, but eventually drifted off around three in the morning.

CHAPTER FOURTEEN

My dream was darker than usual. So dark, it was hard to see the objects around me. I was walking down the stairs of our house. The wallpaper was black, and the furniture was gray, unlike Lily's bright yellow couch and turquoise wallpaper. When I walked outside, I looked around at Lily's garden and the vegetables were rotting.

A strong wind picked up and knocked me to the ground. The breeze caused my hair to dance around in the wind and my eyes to water. I wiped my eyes and when I opened them, I saw color again. I felt the twigs under my knees pierce my skin and the wetness of the grass between my fingers. I stood up and turned around in a full circle. I gasped. My mind was no longer in my dreams. I had sleepwalked out of my room and outside into Lily's front yard garden.

As I walked back toward the house, I heard the cracking of the leaves behind me.

Oh God!

I felt their presence and I could hear them breathing heavily. The hairs on my arms stood straight up and I clenched my fist, ready to throw a punch at whoever it was. I slowly turned around, expecting to face my attacker, but no one was there.

A low growl echoed in my ears and that's when I saw him. His yellow eyes opened, and his body was crouched low. He had four legs, sharp fangs, and course hair, dark as midnight. This wasn't a human, but a large and angry wolf.

He crept toward me, never taking his eyes off mine, and stalked around me, shadowing my movements.

I screamed for help in my mind, but I realized it was pointless. I couldn't scream out loud. The sound of my voice might freak the wolf out and then he would attack. The wolf crept ten feet from me and I shivered. His eyes were still fixed on mine. I tried to assess my situation and determine if there were any move I could make to escape this beast, but all roads led to me being attacked. There was nowhere I could run. I scanned the ground for a weapon.

Help! Someone! Help!

I held up my hands, prepared to use my powers to fend him off, but I was shaking so much that I couldn't focus enough for anything to happen. I had the power to stop him, but I had frozen. I couldn't think straight and my hands became numb and shook violently.

The wolf howled louder, then slowly backed up and moved to my right, allowing me to now have access to run toward the front door. Was he letting me go?

The wolf stopped moving now and glared into my eyes, no longer showing me his teeth. He looked up and took position again. Suddenly, I heard noises coming from the trees around me. They sounded like someone or something large was running in my direction.

Oh, please tell me he didn't call his buddies to help him out.

The sounds grew louder and faster. It sounded like more than one person or thing was running in my direction.

The wolf backed away again but kept his eyes on mine. The sound of running on the twigs and leaves stopped behind me. I turned around to see who had come to my rescue, or to kill me, but my fear only increased as I saw a pack of fisher cats standing behind me in the attack position. Fisher cats weren't exactly the kindest wild animal in Rhode Island. I now didn't know which I was more scared of, as I was surrounded by several animals that could rip me up within seconds.

The fisher cats growled so loudly, it caused me to back up in fear, tripping over a large rock, and fall to the ground. I braced myself for the fall and slowly scooted back toward a tree, staring at these creatures that were now facing each other, ready for battle.

The wolf glared at the fisher cats, showing his teeth. The fisher cats were no longer looking at me but approached the wolf instead. They formed a barricade around me, protecting me, while letting out loud, aggressive growls.

"We heard your call," I heard in my head.

I looked around. "Who's there?"

I've lost my mind.

It wasn't a human voice and no words were being spoken out loud, but for some weird reason, I understood it perfectly. Did I just hear one of the cats talking to me telepathically?

I decided that at this point, anything was possible, so I looked at them intently and focused my mind, trying to force my thoughts in their direction. I wasn't sure if they could hear me back, but it was worth a try.

"Help me."

"Run," I heard another voice say, in my mind.

I didn't have time to question my sanity right now. I did as the cats commanded, ran toward the front door, and slammed it behind me. After locking the door, I ran to the window and looked out at the side yard. The cats were attacking the wolf and he was barely able to defend himself. The cats then backed off and the wolf ran back into the forest, limping from the attack. One of the cats looked up at me and the pack took off running.

My heart was pounding inside my chest. I took a seat on the bench next to the window.

This night is never going to end.

I looked up at the clock and it was six in the morning. Lily would be waking up any minute.

I heard footsteps coming down the stairs.

"You're up early," Lily called out as she made her way down the stairs, tightening her robe around her.

"I couldn't sleep." I walked over to the coffee maker and brewed our morning pick-me-up.

"Coffee?" I asked her, though I already knew the answer.

"Please." She looked at me skeptically. "Mercy, what happened?" Unable to hide anything from her, I told her about Cami's accident and about the sleepwalking that had led me to the animals. Lily tried her best not to show how scared she was, but I could tell. I probably shouldn't have told her all of it, but she couldn't help me while being left in the dark.

Lily had to head to the café to open it up, so I splashed some water on my face and got dressed. A knock at the door startled me. Before I reached the door, I looked at my phone and saw two text messages.

Shannon: *We're coming over.*

Caleb: *I'm not going to text this. Let me explain what you saw. Call me, please.*

I was not going to call him back.

When I opened the door, Riley and Shannon were standing on my porch.

"Come on in."

"You look like hell," Shannon said bluntly as they came through the doorway.

"Um, thanks?" She didn't have much of a filter.

"I called the hospital this morning." Shannon's voice was shaky. "There's been no change with Cami. The doctors are still telling us they don't know when she'll wake up." She threw her hands up in the air. "It doesn't make any sense. There's a railing all the way up the cliff. For Cami to fall, she had to be climbing on the cliff railing and dangling over. She wasn't drunk and she hates heights. Someone threw her. I know it."

My stomach dropped to my knees. Someone did throw her over, but I couldn't tell her what I knew.

"They aren't going to investigate, either," Shannon continued. "They say it's a clear case of drinking, slipping, and falling. Mrs. Thompson wouldn't let the investigators do a blood test for alcohol. They are just assuming. It's bullshit. We saw her right before we got to the beach. She wasn't drinking and she doesn't do drugs."

Riley opened his mouth to say something, but I stopped him with a discreet head shake. His mouth closed and he creased his brow. He knew my secrets, so he would need to know this one.

I knew I was going to regret this. "Maybe we don't know her as well as we thought." Shannon stared at me like I had just killed her dog. Riley shook his head at me and turned his head away.

I hated what I had just said, but she needed to leave this alone. I couldn't risk her digging into her accident. If she did, whoever had hurt Cami could go after her.

"What are you trying to say?" Shannon asked me.

I could barely look at her. My eyes shifted over to Riley, who looked at her briefly and then back to me.

"Shannon, people hide secrets all the time," he added and my heart shattered. I didn't just tell Riley my secrets last night. He was now involved in this life. Shannon walked up to me, tears in her eyes, and let out a hard sob.

"She wasn't on drugs. She wouldn't do that." She glared at both Riley and me for an uncomfortable ten seconds or so. "I'm out of here," she said, choking back her tears.

My heart sank, and I couldn't hold back my own tears any longer. She walked to the door, and forcefully slammed it behind her.

"Was it another witch?" Riley asked.

"We don't know for sure," I said, wiping my eyes. "But whoever it is, they are coming after me and I have to stop them."

There was another knock. I scurried to the front door and looked through the peep hole. Caleb was standing there, running his hands through his hair, looking frustrated.

I cracked the door open and glared at him dramatically. "Caleb, there's a reason I am not responding to your text."

"Let me in, Mercy." He slammed his hand on the door and I jumped back.

He wasn't going to let this go.

"Fine." I didn't want a heated argument today. I was way too tired for this. "But you can say whatever it is in front of Riley. He knows everything." I opened the door the rest of the way and Riley was standing there looking uncomfortable.

"I'll explain tonight, but not here. Not in front of him." He glanced over at Riley. "You really shouldn't have told him. He'll never accept this part of you. Besides, it's dangerous to involve people who don't have the powers we have."

I looked over my shoulder and Riley had taken a seat on the couch, no longer looking our way.

"Okay, when?"

"Tonight. We'll have dinner at my aunt's house in Newport. That's where I've been staying."

I realized I had never asked him where he lived. I was curious now.

"Your aunt? I didn't know you had family out here," I said, surprised.

"You'll like her." He smiled, cutting through the tension in the room. "I'll pick you up at six."

So, his aunt was either a great aunt times ten, or she had done an immortal spell as well.

I'll find out tonight. I'd better find out everything tonight.

CHAPTER FIFTEEN

I glanced at the clock. Caleb would be here any minute. I was wearing denim jeans and a red T-shirt with my hair in a ponytail. I wasn't going to dress up for Caleb tonight. This was certainly not a date. The doorbell rang just as the minute hand struck twelve. Right on time.

I opened the door to see Caleb dressed in a black button-up shirt and gray slacks. His hair fell slightly over his eyes from the heavy wind outside. His messy hair only complemented his breathtaking eyes and gorgeous features.

Focus, Mercy. This isn't a date.

A slight satisfaction hit me, knowing my casual attire would bother him.

"This isn't a date," I said.

"We can make it a date. I dressed up in my best and everything." He flashed me his sexy smile and I rolled my eyes. He was hot, but oh so arrogant.

"Mercy, who is it?" Lily shouted from the family room.

"It's Riley. We're heading to a movie. I'll call you when I'm on my way back," I shouted back.

He smiled. "Good. She would never let you go with me."

I hated lying to Lily, but it was true. She wouldn't let me go anywhere with him, that was for sure.

He held out his hand. "Shall we?" I took his hand in mine and he escorted me out of the house to his car.

We drove across the bridge to Newport and past the mansions into a gated community. We hit a fork in the road and turned left through a beautiful garden trail that led up to a castle, which looked like something out of a fairytale. We took a right into a long driveway that was surrounded by tall trees hovering over the pathway. He parked and rushed over to my side to open the door for me.

"Thanks." I grabbed his hand and stepped out. "What is this place? Is this her house?" I asked.

"This is the Sherwood Remington Castle. My aunt Abigail lives here with her housekeeper, Desiree."

"Is she a great aunt? Or is she immortal too?"

He smiled. "She's immortal."

"So, I knew her?" I was now even more curious.

"Very well." He smiled and gestured toward the massive house. "Shall we?"

I wasn't sure why, but this excited me. I guess meeting those from my past was like me getting to know my original self and a life I was still trying to remember and understand.

I grasped his hand tightly as we entered the castle. I had never seen so many beautiful things all in one setting. Candles were lit on every corner of the house. Beautiful Celtic music was playing in the background and the windows were open to bring in a nice, cool breeze. The window curtains danced in the wind and the gaudy chandelier above the dining room table was dimly lit.

The walls were made of beautiful gold and red silk fabric that looked aged, but still in excellent condition. Beautiful, ornate designs were carved into the wooden posts in the corners of every room. Old furniture from different decades lined the walls. Sculptures, antique china, and rustic books covered the bookshelves that surrounded the foyer. A long, highly-polished oak table sat in the center of the front room with two place settings and wine glasses already set up for us.

Caleb pulled out a chair and gestured for me to sit. He took his seat right as double doors opened from across the room.

A woman dressed in a purple blouse and a black, long skirt entered the room. She looked as if she were in her mid-thirties and she was incredibly beautiful. She had bright blue eyes, flawless pale skin, and wavy blonde hair that fell right above her shoulders.

"Mercy. You look just like ... yourself!" Her eyes widened as she scanned me head to toe. "My goodness. Aside from your hair color, you haven't changed one bit." The way she stared at me made me slightly uncomfortable, so I looked up at Caleb, who only smiled.

"I know you don't have your memories, but we were very close when you were a child. Caleb hasn't stopped talking about how excited he is to have you back."

Caleb gave a shy smile, then chuckled under his breath. Abigail leaned in and gave me a warm, welcoming hug. Caleb moved in slightly as if to stop us and he looked nervous when Abigail touched me. I wondered what was wrong. She looked far from dangerous.

She must be a powerful witch.

"Are you okay, Caleb?" I asked.

"Yes, fine," he assured me with a warm smile before I relaxed.

"It's great to have you in my home, Mercy. You are welcome here any time."

"Thanks." I smiled at her and looked around the dining room again. "Is it just you and your housekeeper here?"

"Desiree," she asserted. We used to work for the man who built this place, Sherwood. He died a few years ago and left me this house as part of an inheritance."

"Wow. That was generous. Well, I appreciate you letting us come here tonight. Whatever is cooking in that kitchen smells lovely."

Lovely? I shuddered at how ridiculous I sounded. I never used words like "lovely".

I noticed that nothing about Abigail looked out of place. She moved around the table to greet Caleb. Her movements were smooth, like she was gliding on ice. I had never met anyone who was so perfectly elegant.

"Your house is so lovely."

I'd said it again. What was wrong with me?

I was starting to feel uncomfortable, so I gave Caleb a pleading look. I straightened up in the chair when Caleb finally spoke with a snicker in his voice.

"What's for dinner tonight, Abigail?" Caleb asked.

I took a deep breath and finally started to relax into the chair.

"Well whatever it is, it smells totally awesome." I said. This time, I made sure I sounded like a teenage delinquent.

Caleb, obviously aware of what I was doing, laughed under his breath.

"Desiree is preparing you two chicken parmesan pasta with a special ingredient of mine. And Caleb knows, I will never tell." Abigail smiled as she grabbed the wine bottle off the table and poured me a glass. "Desiree and I have already eaten, so once dinner has been served, I'll leave you to your date."

"It's not a date." I corrected her. I looked up at Caleb who rolled his eyes at me, and Abigail simply smiled, topping off my glass. "Oh, I know I look older than I am, but I'm only seventeen." I had always wanted to try some of Lily's wine but was too afraid to ask. Taking a glass from Caleb's aunt felt weird.

"It's just for tonight. One glass won't kill you." She smiled and walked to Caleb's side of the table with the bottle.

Again, I didn't want to be rude, so I took a sip and shuddered as it went down. It tasted sweet but had a weird kick and aftertaste. This would take some getting used to.

"Abigail grows the grapes on her property and her staff makes it themselves."

"Well, it's delicious," I lied. "Thank you."

Abigail smiled at me. Then she just stared, causing my heartbeat to pick up.

"Do you remember anything, Mercy, about your life before this?" she asked as she filled up Caleb's glass with the remaining wine in the bottle.

"Only a few memories have come back in visions." I glared at Caleb sternly. He looked uncomfortable. Good. "Caleb is going to help me make sense of it. That's why I'm here tonight."

She smiled again and then turned toward the kitchen as Desiree entered through the entryway.

"Dinner is served. Tonight, we have chicken parmesan with pasta, garden salad, and whole wheat rolls, fresh out of the oven," Desiree said. "Mercy, yours is made with soy protein and topped with our garden's fresh basil."

Abigail's housekeeper was a young girl, maybe fifteen. She was short, with black, pixie-cut hair, a thin frame, pale complexion, and dark green eyes. She wore a white and blue striped sundress, with an off-white lacy apron.

"Hey, Caleb." She then turned to me. "Wow, you sure are beautiful. I'm Desiree."

"Nice to meet you, Desiree. I'm Mercy. Are you also family?"

"Not by blood, but we're pretty much like brother and sister." She playfully punched Caleb in the arm. He grinned and shook his head.

"I'm your waitress for the night. Caleb mentioned you liked pasta and don't eat meat." I looked over at Caleb, who smirked at me.

He was very observant. He had to have been following me for a while before he made his first approach near the park.

"Did I eat meat in my past life?" I asked Caleb.

"You did. You have picked up on new likes and dislikes and have formed quite a different personality, but you're still you."

Desiree smiled and took both our cloth napkins and placed them on our laps.

Caleb and I didn't say much during dinner. I was too nervous about spilling my food on my elegant napkin. It looked more like something you would hang on a wall than something anyone would use to wipe food from their face.

Abigail had excused herself along with Desiree while he and I ate.

After dinner, Desiree cleared the table and Caleb grabbed my hand and lifted me up from the chair. "Dance with me?"

Caleb, acting like a gentleman, escorted me across the dining area and to the room behind us. As we entered through the double doors, I heard beautiful violin music playing over the speakers surrounding the room.

"You used to be a fantastic dancer." He took a bow while gesturing toward me.

"Yeah, but in this life, I have zero rhythm," I joked.

"You used to dance with me all the time." He tenderly grabbed my hand and pulled me in closer to him and I tensed. As charming as he was right now, I knew what he was doing and I didn't have time for it.

"I need answers, Caleb. You're stalling."

"I'm going to tell you everything, Mercy, but I miss this. One dance." He closed the space between us, nuzzling his cheek next to mine. "Just one dance."

He wanted us to be like we used to be. This wasn't about dancing. This was about what we used to have over three hundred years ago.

He smiled and grabbed my arms, intertwining his left hand with my right and his right hand fell down and relaxed on my waist. His touch sent chills down my spine.

He kept a good distance between us as he positioned himself for the waltz.

"I know what you're doing, Caleb."

"Do you?"

I was done waiting. I released our stance, pulled him by the collar toward my body forcefully, and placed my lips on his. Sure, I was doing the very thing I blasted him across the driveway for doing, but this wasn't about games or desire. This was about finding answers.

The kiss made my entire body melt and ache for his touch. The moment was short lived, as my mind then drew me into another vision, just as I suspected it would.

Caleb and I were standing over a woman who was lying on the floor. She was begging us to let her go. He grabbed a handful of her hair and dragged her as she was kicking and screaming for him to release her.

What was he doing?

"Caleb, let go of her. Let me talk to her!" I screamed at him in the vision.

He threw her onto a pile of bodies, lifted his hands, and flames appeared. He leaned down and touched their bodies, causing the flames to erupt around them. The screams were unlike anything I had ever heard.

I saw myself close my eyes and begin sobbing. It was clear I hadn't wanted any of that to happen.

I ended the kiss abruptly and backed up, causing the memory to disappear.

"Shit," he cursed. He must have seen the fear on my face. It was clear I had seen something bad. Something he didn't want me to know about.

"Don't move." I held up my hands.

Just then, Abigail walked into the ballroom.

"Mercy, you should go now. Caleb don't try and stop her."

Caleb didn't say another word but he breathed heavily, watching me back away from him.

I said nothing, either, as I turned and ran out of the ballroom, grabbed my purse hanging from my dining chair, and exited the castle. I opened my Driver app to request a ride home and stood at the end of the driveway waiting for them, shaking from the cold and more intensely, from my nerves. Tears flooded my face as I had trouble breathing.

I'm such a fool to have trusted him.

Were Abigail and Desiree safe? I turned around and contemplated heading back in the house, but she must have known what I was thinking. She was so quick to enter the room as if she knew I had discovered Caleb's darkest secret and she was trying to protect me from a murderer. I thought at first, maybe it was me that was the killer, but I was begging him to stop; I didn't want the woman in the vision to die. He was trying to control me now, just like he had done back then. I was just a little soldier.

What didn't make sense was that he had told me I was the coven leader. But if I were, then he would have listened to me when I told him to stop, but he didn't. What did that woman do to deserve being burned alive? There were so many bodies burning from his own hands.

My driver arrived, and we headed toward my home. I cried the entire way and ignored my ringtone. It was slightly after ten before I got home and quietly snuck back into my room.

Aside from that horrible vision I had tonight, I was still nowhere near having the answers I needed. Tonight had not gone as I had planned.

I need to think of another way to get my memories back.

CHAPTER SIXTEEN

As I laid in bed last night, I thought a lot about what to do next. I didn't trust Caleb enough to know if he was being completely truthful, and even as good looking as he was, I really didn't want to kiss him every time I needed to see a glimpse of my past. I did some research online on the topic of paganism and witchcraft, and a witch shop in Providence popped up on the top search. It's not exactly what I thought I'd be doing, but I didn't know what else to do.

I looked up at Patricia's Witch Shop, just north of Providence.

What am I doing?

"Good morning, darling. Welcome," an older woman said as I entered. She was wearing a long blue dress, and her gray hair was wrapped in a yellow silk scarf. "Don't be shy. Come on in."

Seriously, what am I doing?

She stalked around me and picked up a globe sitting on a shelf next to the entrance. She smiled and walked to the back, disappearing behind a curtain. Several books lined a shelf along the side wall. I worked my way to the back and scanned over them. Most of the books were novels about witches and the supernatural, but a few were non-fiction books about the history of witchcraft.

"Is there something in particular you're looking for?" she asked from behind me, startling me.

"Honestly, I don't know." I giggled softly to myself, turning my attention back to the books. "I don't even know if you have what I need."

She tilted her head and slowly closed her eyes, took a breath in, and opened them back up. "You seek answers, but you're afraid of what you'll find?" she asked.

I quickly turned my attention back to her. She was still holding the globe in her hand. "Are you a psychic?" I asked.

"I am. I can do a reading for you. I'm just setting up my table for a client, but they won't be here for another fifteen minutes, so I have time."

I shook my head, "Naw, I'm okay," I responded, eyeing the bookshelf again, "What about spell books? Are these books authentic?"

She walked past me and placed her hand on the shelf, closing her eyes again and gliding her fingers across each book until she stopped. "This one is from 1725. I found it during my travels in Europe a few years ago. It's not for anyone, though. I can't give this to you unless I do a reading."

"You really want to do a reading on me, huh?"

All she did was smile at me, while pulling the book from the shelf. She turned her back to me and walked to the backroom again, behind the curtain.

Okay. That was weird.

I looked once again at the books on the shelf, but nothing stood out to me. I turned back around and browsed around the shop. Over in the corner were racks with herbs and stones. I spotted the sage and picked up three of them and a few jet stones. These probably had no powers like the one on my necklace but it didn't hurt to have a few extra on me. I placed them on the counter by the register and rang the bell. She didn't come. I rang it again but only heard her clearing her throat in the back.

Guess I'm doing this.

Once I pushed through the curtain, she was sitting at a round table with a red sheet over it and in the center was the globe.

When I looked more closely at her, I saw her eyes were closed while her left hand was placed on top of the book she grabbed from the shelf.

"You want me to sit right there?" I gestured to the chair across from her. She didn't answer, so I sat down anyway. She opened her eyes which were now as white as snow. I gasped and my heartbeat picked up.

"I dreamed about you last night. I knew you were coming," she said.

Is this a parlor trick?

"Can I just please buy that book? I'll pay double just so that I don't have to do a reading."

Her eyes turned back to brown and it calmed me. "You came here for answers, did you not?"

I nodded. "I don't believe in psychics. Sorry."

"Ah, you used to not believe in witches, either," she said, while rubbing the top of the book. She opened it up, flipping through several pages, and stopped. "You're an old soul. This spell will help you remember."

My heart raced. How could she know that? "You're not a psychic, are you? You're a witch."

"I'm a witch that can see the future. So yes, I am also psychic. I don't know anything about your life before this. Your soul now is only bound to this body and this life. My dream last night simply showed you showing up at my shop and that you seek to understand your purpose. That, I can help with. Let me do a reading."

I looked down at her hand that was still by the spell book and she lightly tapped her fingers on the pages.

"What do I need to do?" I asked and reached out my hand. "Are you going to read my palm or something?"

She shook her head while her other hand grabbed a stack of cards that I now noticed were next to her globe. "I'm going to draw tarot cards."

"Okay." I gave her an agreeable nod.

She shuffled the cards a few times and then closed her eyes again. "Mind and body, life once well. Memories taken, hear this spell. Take her mind and make it whole. Return the life that death hath stole." She pulled the top card over and displayed a blade. "Your journey never ended; it's only just begun," she explained. "You were a warrior. You need to train again. You need to seek guidance from someone you are running from. You can trust them."

I assumed she was referring to Caleb. I looked at the blade more steadily. It wasn't shiny gray like a kitchen knife. It was possibly carved from a tree. It looked very much like the one from my vision that Caleb had been sharpening.

She flipped the next card. It was a red heart, outlined in black. "You loved someone once, but you lost them tragically."

My death.

She flipped the next card. On it was a swirled circle that started out large and then became smaller until it met in the middle of the card with a green triangle encasing it. I hadn't looked at it longer than a few seconds before I felt my eyes roll to the back of my head and my inner thoughts opening to a world around me.

In it, I *saw* a woman I somehow knew was my mother from my past life, holding me in her arms. A midwife was wiping me down with a wet rag and wrapping me in a white blanket.

"We will call her Mercy," my mother said to the man I knew as my father.

The scenes flipped past quickly, like scenes in an old-timey projector. First there was an infant me, crying in a bassinet, while my mother cried into my father's arms saying she wasn't good enough.

Good enough for what?

Next, I saw my childhood friends: Caleb, Simon, Ezra, and Leah. I saw myself grow to love them as my family. Next, I was standing in a room with instructors teaching us how to fight. I threw punches at a man I knew as Caleb's father, Roland. I turned around to see someone I had no emotional connection with running toward me.

"Turn around, Mercy," Roland ordered, throwing me a stake.

A stake?

As I turned around, I felt a blunt force slam into my chest as this other man threw me to the ground. I wrestled with him, gripping the stake.

"Mercy, now! What are you waiting for?" Roland screamed.

I gripped the stake as hard as I could and plunged the stake into his chest. The body of this man exploded on top of me, covering me in brown ash.

"Wake up."

My eyes shot open when I heard her voice.

"Oh my God," I gasped.

"What did you see?" she asked.

"The symbol had triggered the visions from my past life. I've had visions before, but nothing like this. I had felt things and touched things. I remember a huge part of my life back then." I pointed to the symbol on the card. "What does this mean?"

She looked at me with fear in her eyes. "It means vampire hunter."

Before I left the shop, Patricia explained how witches had heard about a special coven that were sent to Earth centuries ago, but the history books never explained about their purpose in fighting vampires. They only knew that each witch carried a special power that would help other witches manifest their own. They had only heard tales that vampires once existed, but vampires hadn't been seen since the Salem trials.

The unsettled feeling of my vision came over me as I sat in my car in front of her shop. Fighting vampires wasn't a small part in the history of my past life; it was the reason for my existence.

My phone beeped and I looked down to see who it was.

Shannon: *Meet me at Riley's. He was attacked by an animal last night.*

My heart pounded into overdrive against my chest.

Me: *I'm on my way.*

Not Riley. Please God, please help him be ok.

When I arrived, Shannon was waiting in the driveway for me.

"I texted you." I inched toward her. "I'm so sorry for what I said. I didn't mean it."

She caught me off guard with a warm hug. "I know you didn't mean what you said. You're just upset. We all are."

I squeezed my arms around her and released our hug. "Let's go in," I said.

As we filed into the kitchen, Mr. Davis told us what had happened.

"Yesterday morning when he was heading back from your house, he stopped by Goddard Park to take our boat out. He was found by a girl going for a run. She found him lying on the parking lot with a huge bite mark on his leg. There was so much blood. She rushed him to the hospital. The hospital released him a few hours later, but this morning, Riley was complaining about feeling sick."

Animal attack? I thought about the wolf that tried to attack me.

I looked up at Mr. Davis as it dawned on me. "Did Riley say what kind of animal it was that attacked him?"

"He said it was hard to tell because it was so dark but he said it looked like a wolf. There aren't any in these parts, so I figured it could have just been a big black dog. He was really shaken up about it. I also thought maybe one of those damn fisher cats."

I shuddered. "Can we go see him now?"

"Yeah, go on up."

We heard Riley calling out to us; his voice sounded weak. We walked in and Riley was curled up on his bed in the fetal position, holding his stomach.

"He's been like this since this morning," his dad explained.

"What's wrong with him? Didn't they do tests to make sure the animal that attacked him didn't have rabies? Could it be that?" Shannon asked.

"They tested him. We will have his blood work back in a few days. I don't think he'd have symptoms this fast, so maybe an infection, though his wound today doesn't look nearly as bad as it did after he was attacked. He has been throwing up and his temperature spiked to 104. The doctor doesn't think it's related to the attack, more like symptoms of the flu. If it gets worse by the end of the day, I'm to bring him back in."

I walked up to Riley and put my hand on his head. "You're so warm."

Mr. Davis grabbed a wet cloth from the bathroom and handed it to me. I placed it over his forehead. "Here, this should cool you down." I rubbed the back of my hand over his cheek.

"Riley, talk to me. I am sorry we weren't here earlier. We didn't know," I said.

Riley smiled at me and placed his hand on my hand. "It's okay, Mercy. Thanks for coming over." His voice was strained.

I couldn't hold back the tears. I hated seeing him like this. A tear fell on Riley's hand and he wiped it off.

"Sorry." We both chuckled, but I was still crying.

"Stop crying, Mercy. This isn't your fault." He wiped one of my tears away. Riley then looked at Shannon. "Thanks for coming, guys, but I'll be okay. I don't want you two getting sick, so I'll just call you once I'm better. Hopefully before the game."

"The game?" I asked, but then remembered. I had completely forgotten. "Are we still doing it, with everything that has happened this week, with Cami?"

"That's exactly why we're still doing it. Cami loves these games. She'd want us to still go," he said.

Every summer since I was a freshman, my friends and I had gathered together, snuck onto our school's football field, and played flag football to celebrate the ending of a school year. We had graduated, so this would be our last summer game.

We all smiled and gave him a nod. "I'll call you later to check on you."

I scooted closer to Riley and he gave me a side smirk. "Don't worry about me, okay? I'm sure this will pass in a few days."

I grabbed his hand and squeezed it lightly. "I'll see you at the game."

CHAPTER SEVENTEEN

Two days had passed since my vision about being a vampire hunter. I woke up overwhelmed by everything that had happened in the last few weeks. I should have been excited about today, but I wasn't. Today was my birthday.

I couldn't stop thinking about the man I had killed and the woman Caleb threw into the pile of bodies in my memories. It all made sense now.

They were vampires.

Vampires! I still was having a hard time wrapping my mind around the fact that vampires existed. Were they all evil? Did they all deserve to die?

Caleb had tried calling me yesterday numerous times, but I didn't pick up. He wasn't my enemy, I knew that now, but I also knew if I faced him about this and let him know what I saw, everything would change. If he knew that I knew everything, it would no longer be a memory. It would be my life.

The game was tonight and I honestly didn't want to see anyone. But like Riley had said, Cami loved these games. She would want me there, smiling and cheering on our friends.

I went downstairs and Lily had just finished up breakfast, placing her plate in the sink.

I drew a photo of the symbol I had seen from the tarot card on a piece of paper and set it down on the table. "Do you know what this means?" I asked.

She shook her head, "No. Where did you see that?"

"I went to a witch shop yesterday in Providence. A witch, who's also a psychic, pulled a tarot card with this symbol on it. Looking at the image brought my memories back. In one of those memories, I saw myself kill a vampire. The symbol means vampire hunter," I said, now taking a seat at the kitchen table.

Her eyes shot open. "Whoa."

"Yeah, that's basically what I'm feeling right now. I'm feeling a mix of shock, fear, and relief. It means I didn't kill a human in my visions. I was a vampire hunter, Lily. I wasn't fighting thieves and murderers, I was fighting the undead." I sighed and leaned forward now, pressing my elbows on the table. "Did you know they existed?"

"I've never met one, but I heard the stories. They have all gone into hiding, though. At least that's what Joel told me. I didn't know that was what you were fighting in your past life. Your mom didn't say they were vampires, just that you fought evil that was threatening our ancestors. For all we knew, that could have been witches using black magic"

"I'm scared, Lily. If this is my destiny, I can't escape it. Caleb wants me to perform an immortal spell. I can't do that."

"That won't happen," she said firmly. "I won't let him make you immortal."

This is when I realized she was the only one in my corner. She would protect me no matter what, and I had to let her in.

Lily gestured to my phone. "Call Joel. He'll fly back out."

"I don't want to burden him. He was just here."

"He can help you. If you ever need someone to talk to, he's someone that does actively use his magic. He can teach you how to control your powers, much better than I can."

She was right. Caleb knew more about my powers than anyone, so it made sense for him to be the one to teach me, but I didn't trust him completely, not yet. I needed my family right now.

Joel was able to catch a flight out early enough so he could be here by the time I went through my Awakening. I spent the day home doing absolutely nothing, which was nice. Lily came back around five from working at the café all day and made us some spaghetti. Joel got to our place right around the same time, and together they sang Happy Birthday to me, and I blew out my eighteen candles.

"Thanks, guys." I looked at the clock on my phone. "Shoot, I need to get to the game. I'll be back by ten, at the latest. You guys can prep me before I go through my transition."

"It's really not a huge ordeal, just a little overwhelming. It will mostly feel like a stream of water is entering your body, but you can breathe it in without drowning. For you, it might be different because your powers are a lot different than any of ours. We will be right by your side," he assured me.

Lily grabbed a card from the counter and handed it over to me. "Happy birthday, Mercy. Now, go be a kid for the next few hours. There's a gift card in there." She grabbed my hand and squeezed. "I will hold your hand tonight as you go through the transition. You won't be alone," she said. It was crazy how calm they seemed. I was so nervous, I felt like throwing up.

I gave her a big hug. "Thank you, Lily. See you guys tonight."

"Make sure you're wearing the jet stone necklace. There is still evil out there and it will protect you. I noticed you don't always wear it. Please, wear it," Lily pleaded.

"I will, I promise."

Lily turned to Joel. "I'm going to shower and then we can head to dinner."

"Where are you guys going?"

"Joe's Bar and Grill," she answered. "It's happy hour." She smiled, turned, and headed upstairs.

Joel leaned back in his chair and smirked. "All right, kiddo. Get out of here."

My phone rang as Joel stood up.

"Hey, Mercy," Riley said when I answered.

"Wow. You sound better. How do you feel?"

"I feel awesome. A few hours after you left, I was myself again."

"Wow. That's weird." I eyed the clock on the wall, seeing that I should head out soon before the game started. "Are you meeting me at the game?"

"Yeah, I'll be there."

"Cool," I said. I need my friend. I needed Riley.

"Look for me in the bleachers. I'm not going to play, so I'll be on the sidelines cheering with you," he said.

Once I arrived, I looked around the larger-than-usual audience, full of rowdy students, until I finally spotted Riley.

"Riley!" I yelled from across the bleachers. He looked at me, smiled, and waved me on up.

"Where's Shannon?" I asked as I reached the seat next to him.

"She's with the other cheerleaders."

I searched the crowd looking for her. I spotted the back of her head, sitting on the lawn, stretching with the rest of the girls.

"Hey, are you doing okay?" he asked.

"Not really. You ready for this?"

"Oh boy, what now?" he said, picking up his fast food burger and taking a bite.

"I figure since you took the news about me being a witch so well, this won't shock you too much."

"There's more?" He asked with his mouth full of food.

"Oh, there's more." I took a deep breath in like I was ready to spill it out in one breath. "So, every time I kiss Caleb, I have these visions. The night he took me to his aunt's house, I saw something horrible when we kissed."

Riley shifted in his seat and looked down.

"Sorry, I should have left that part out. I wasn't thinking," I said, now feeling uncomfortable.

"No, *I'm* sorry. You have every right to kiss someone else."

"But that's the thing, Riley. I just did it to get answers. I knew I'd have another vision."

"It's cool. But keep going. What happened after that?"

"Well, I freaked out and ran out of his aunt's house as fast as I could before he could explain what I had seen. The next day, I went to this witch shop after searching topics online about witchcraft and I found a witch, who's also a psychic, who read three tarot cards for me. One had this strange, triangular symbol on it. The symbol triggered my memories. In one of them, I saw myself stake a man through his heart, and right before my eyes, he turned to dust. The psychic told me the symbol means vampire hunter."

He stared at me expressionless.

"It means I'm a vampire hunter," I repeated.

He continued to stare as if he hadn't heard me.

I laughed, throwing my head back dramatically, like I was losing my mind. "So, there's that."

"Whoa," he said under his breath.

He looked at his burger as if he'd lost his appetite and set it down next to him. "This is intense, Mercy. I mean ... vampire hunter?"

"Yeah, and also since it's my birthday—"

"Happy birthday," he snuck in there.

"Thanks, Riley, but it doesn't really feel like it. My Awakening is tonight, so I'm supposed to become this all-powerful witch. I *am* scared and sort of losing it, but there isn't anything I can do to stop it."

"I will be with you through all of it."

"Thank you. I hope it doesn't freak you out, and I understand if you want nothing to do with me and this life. It's dangerous, Riley."

He grabbed my hand but hesitated at first. When I didn't flinch, he gripped it tighter. "I'm with you until the end," he promised.

The end. If only he knew I didn't have an end. This was only the beginning for me.

The game had now started. The teams were determined by the first letter of their first name to make things fair, as there was a mix of all four classes on the field.

An hour went by and each time a team scored a touchdown, Riley and I would jump up and cheer.

The game was now coming to an end as Jeff Yung was running to win the final touchdown. As he reached the end of the field, he tripped on the turf and his leg bent under him. The cheers turned to screams and shouts as Jeff lay on the field, with an obvious broken limb.

Jeff was the ground crying out for help and his body was trembling as if he were having a seizure.

Riley was calling 911 as I ran toward the field. I didn't even hesitate, I knew I could help him. When I reached the field, my eyes were fixed on him, with one goal in mind—heal him.

When I reached Jeff, I knelt and placed my hand on his chest. He was shaking so badly, but the moment my hand touched him, he calmed.

"Back up!" I shouted to the students gathering around him.

"Please, give him space." They backed up, and I hovered over Jeff, shielding everyone from seeing what I was about to do. Jeff looked up at me and my hand lingered down to his leg. "Don't move, okay?" I whispered.

I closed my eyes and felt the energy flow through my body like waves rolling over each other and onto a shore. My fingers warmed as the energy left my body and entered Jeff. His light brown eyes, for a moment, turned a shade of green and he looked up at me, shock and disbelief read over his face. "There," I said as I let go.

Jeff sat up and bent his leg. "I ..." he started to say. I shook my head at him. "Mercy, did you just ...?"

I shook my head again. "Jeff, you fell and sprained your ankle. That's what happened right?" I told him, insinuating the lie.

His eyes grew wide and he came to his feet, helping me to mine. "Yes, of course, I guess it just hurt worse than it really was." He gave me an agreeable nod, while a couple of his guy friends were now by his side.

"Dude, what happened?" James asked.

"Hey, at least I made the touchdown," he boasted, giving me one last worrisome look.

The guys all slapped hands and everyone started to cheer. Jeff gave me one more look of disbelief. He had witnessed a miracle, and I was sure I'd have to give him more of an explanation later.

Oh, please don't say anything, Jeff. You owe me for this one.

As I turned around to look up at Riley to see if he was still on the bleachers, I ran into someone's chest. I looked up. My heart pounded so hard, I felt like it was going to leap out of my chest. I looked into Caleb's eyes.

CHAPTER EIGHTEEN

"Caleb? What are you doing here?"

"That was careless, Mercy," he scolded me like I was a child as he looked over at Jeff. "You can't just go around healing anyone you want. It's dangerous. If people knew what you could do—"

"I couldn't just watch him suffer. He broke his femur."

I knew Caleb was right and I hated that he was. I put myself and the coven at risk. I don't know what I was thinking, but knowing I had the power to heal him and not do anything also didn't feel right.

Caleb sighed deeply and looked up at Riley on the bleachers. "Did you drive with him? Or is your car here?"

"My car is here. Why?"

"I need you to do the Awakening in Danvers, not at your home. There is more to the spell that must happen, that Lily and Joel can't be a part of. I also need to bind you to the coven, so I need to be there."

"Then we can go pick up Lily and Joel. They're at Joe's Bar and Grill. Let me go get Riley."

"No, you won't," Caleb snarled through gritted teeth.

"Caleb, stop. If it's absolutely necessary that I do this somewhere else with you, they won't stand in the way. I need them there—"

His hands were on my head before I could speak another word, and my eyes rolled back to darkness.

~

When I opened my eyes, we were pulling up to a little cottage in a wooded area.

He parked the car and I glared at him until he looked at me. "You kidnapped me? Are you kidding?"

He turned off the ignition without responding.

I looked down at my phone, which he thankfully hadn't taken from me, and I had six missed phone calls between Riley, Lily and Joel.

"Can I at least call them and let them know I'm okay? They'll worry sick." I pleaded, hoping he'd understand. "*Am* I okay?"

"I'm not going to hurt you. You know that. But just text them," he said. He shook his head slightly and gripped the steering wheel. "I'm not trying to be difficult, but we don't have time for you to call them. You know how that call will play out."

I was still pissed at him for taking me against my will, but he was right. Lily would just freak out and this whole ordeal would become more dramatic than it needed to be. Even if I did ask for their help, or try to run, I would never make it back to East Greenwich on time, and then I'd be alone during the Awakening.

I group-texted Lily and Joel first.

Me: *I'm with Caleb. I'm safe*

My hands felt clammy. I hated lying to everyone. Maybe I was safe, but I sure didn't feel like it. I scrolled through my messages until I found the last message I sent Riley.

Me: *Hey Riley, I know you saw Caleb take me. I'm safe. I'll call you once I go through my Awakening.*

I kept it simple. Any extra details about why he took me would just set off an alarm of worry between the three of them.

After I texted everyone that I was "safe" with Caleb, I turned my phone down and put it in my pocket. We got out of the car and entered the home through the front door and I could smell the ash from a recently burned log in the fireplace. The cottage felt warm and inviting. It was filled with old furniture and ancient sculptures. There was a collection of artifacts that looked centuries old covering the shelves against the walls and paintings that reached from the floor to the ceiling.

"Whose place is this?" I asked as we walked over to the couch.

"It's mine," he answered with an unreadable expression on his face.

I sat down on his couch and looked around the room. This cottage wasn't what I expected. The truth was that I didn't really know what I had expected. I could maybe picture it as a family home, parents and children laughing and playing games, not as the dwelling place of a powerful flame-throwing witch.

He stepped toward me when he entered the family room and looked down at me. "I know you don't agree with my methods and I've kept things from you, but I did it to help you learn who you are. We grew up learning about our powers from childhood. You didn't have that in this new life. I had to tread lightly with you, so you could use your powers the way you're supposed to. We don't use spell books. We act on instinct, and with you not understanding what was happening to you, it was shielding you from that. Tonight, with you helping that guy on the field, you knew you had to save him, and you did, even though it was a really stupid thing to do." He glared at me and I just squinted my eyes at him stubbornly.

I walked over to the couch and turned to him. "I know I'm a vampire hunter. Or, or at least, I used to be."

His eyebrows rose a notch. "I've been trying to tell you the last few times we've seen each other, but you kept running from me." He paused. "How did you find out?"

"A psychic showed me on a tarot card." I smiled, proud of myself for not needing his help.

He wasn't smiling back. "Mercy!"

"Look, it doesn't matter how I found out. But I know now. I have all my memories from birth to about the age of twelve or thirteen. It came to me when I looked at the symbol on the tarot card." I shook my head. "I don't want to kill people, Caleb."

"They're not people." He tried to explain it to me, but I just shook my head again and sat down on the couch.

He sat next to me and looked down, brushing the hair from the sides of my face and away from my eyes. "You're not a murderer."

"I was. Whether it was a vampire or a human, I still took a life."

Caleb shook his head and ran his hands through his hair. "There is more to this story," he said.

"I'm ready to hear it. I need to know everything. I don't care what I see, I'm not running."

His voice was calm and steady. "Centuries ago, an angel came down to Earth. She was sent to stop a demon from destroying the human race. Instead, she fell in love with him and helped him create the very thing she was sent to stop. Their union created a half breed: part demon, part angel."

"A vampire," I said. "Beauty on the outside, but with a dark and evil soul."

"Vampires don't have souls," he corrected.

"That's unsettling."

"Yeah, and it spread like wildfire. Vampires were creating more vampires, and the destruction was more than the witches on Earth could handle. Our purpose in coming here was to rid the world of them. After you died, we struggled to keep the balance. Our coven went their own ways and we did our best to kill as many as we could on our own." He closed his eyes and drew in a breath. "The feeling of a witch drawing the energy from you is unlike anything else in the world." He opened his eyes.

I was a vessel that was lost to my kind. That must have been horrible for them.

"Why didn't the angel that created me, just bring me back? Surely she had the power to do so."

He shook his head. "We couldn't find your soul, it was as if you died with your body. The first time I felt you after you died, was when the spell worked with your mom. We don't know where you went. My guess is, neither did the angel." He grabbed my hand gently. "When you go through the Awakening, you will be a tool for all the witches in this world. You're going to help them. We can't do this without you."

He held up his hand and instantly a flame appeared on the tip of his thumb. "When a witch draws the powers of Fire using my element, I give that to them, no questions asked." He shut his hand and the flame disappeared.

"What does Spirit actually do?" I asked.

"Spirit is a little bit different than the rest. You bind all our powers together. You control the power of healing, nature, and telepathy. When you died years ago, the power to heal someone was taken from this earth. It was the key to what the power of Spirit represented. Witches haven't been able to heal anyone for centuries. We needed that power, but it was gone. When I brought you back, we could all feel that power again, but your mom began to shield it from us. Once you awaken, we can do so much more with your gifts."

I thought back about my childhood and how I knew I was different. It brought a feeling of sadness and anger that my mom had hidden this part of me. The people I could have helped, the lives I could have saved, were non-existent because of her.

Caleb continued. "Part of Spirit is that you can move objects with your mind and telepathically speak to someone. My guess is this is how you can talk to animals today. Your powers must be heightened in this new life."

"So, if I want to move water, I can do it without pulling it from Leah, but other witches would have to pull that energy from her?"

"Yes."

"This is crazy," I said.

He placed the back of his hand on my cheek. "And amazing." He smiled at me and lightly brushed my cheek with his hand. I moved back, releasing his touch from my cheek.

"You kidnapped me, Caleb. How do you expect me to trust you when you treat me like that?"

"I would never hurt you, but I also know what's best for you. You don't have your memories and you don't truly understand what's at stake. I can't have Lily and Joel trying to stop what we need to do. They don't understand, either," he explained, but it didn't make me any less irritated by how he had handled the situation.

He didn't touch me again, but he inched closer to my side.

"You were destined to fight evil and save other witches from being destroyed by the demons that were created to kill them. The angel couldn't destroy her own child, but she hated what she had helped create."

I had read a few books about vampires and werewolves, but never did I suspect anything like this could be real. I searched my thoughts. "What else is real? Dracula?"

Caleb snickered. "Fiction."

"Frankenstein?" I always tried to be funny when I was nervous, but this time, I was serious. If witches and vampires were real, what else could be real?

"Fiction."

"So, I killed a vampire." I hoped saying it out loud would make me feel better about what I had done, but I still felt sick about it.

"I couldn't just come out and tell you everything in your room the first time we talked. It would have overwhelmed you. You discovering it through your visions wasn't exactly how I wanted it to play out, either, but now you know."

"Now I know." I looked up at the ceiling and rubbed my eyes. The lack of sleep the last few nights was getting to me. "What did the vampire I killed do to deserve death?" I asked.

"That vampire had just slaughtered an entire village. Women and children were killed and bodies were left to rot on the streets. You were protecting the humans. You were a hero, not a killer."

It felt a little bit better hearing that. Just a little.

"And the woman you killed in my vision? The people you burned alive?"

He closed his eyes tightly and balled his fist. "She and her blood-sucking clan killed my mother, turned my father into one of them, and took your father prisoner."

I quickly sat up and looked at him in disbelief.

Oh my God.

He looked so upset, as if he were living it all over again. "I was so angry for what they had done, I had to kill her. I had to make them pay."

His eyes watered, but he wouldn't allow the tears to fall. This was the first time I had seen Caleb this sad. It was strange to see him so broken.

"Why did I try and stop you?"

"Because we didn't know where they were taking your father. You thought if we kept her alive, we could torture her for answers, but I couldn't stop myself. You hated her just as much as I did, but you wanted me to stop so we could find your father. For that, I am so sorry, Mercy."

"Did you ever find him?"

"No. We searched, but we couldn't find him."

The feeling of anxiety tightened in my chest. I had to steady my breathing. He had killed children. I did what I had to do. Right?

"Is that everything?" I still felt like he was holding something back.

"Your blood is very powerful to a vampire. It makes them much stronger and will allow them to walk in the light, so once you go through the Awakening, they'll come after you."

I gulped. This was a new twist. "Why are you just now telling me this?"

"This isn't something I could have just dropped on you until you had a full grasp of your purpose here."

I studied his face. I could see it in his eyes that he was holding back again. He shifted uncomfortably in his seat, and I understood why.

"That's why you kidnapped me. You knew Lily and Joel would stop you. You're going to make me immortal."

"You being a mortal is a problem, Mercy. You're going to be hunted. They know I brought you back. They know what will happen tonight after you turn eighteen. If you get caught, some will not be able to stop when they drink your blood and it will kill you. I need you alive." Caleb bowed his head. "I won't lose you again."

"I don't know if I can watch the people I love die while I continue to live. Living forever, that's a big deal, Caleb." I collected my thoughts and went over in my mind if there was any other way. If I died, the element that was crucial for the survival of the witches would be gone again, but if I became immortal, I would watch Lily, Joel, and my friends die, and I would be fighting demons for eternity.

Caleb pulled me out of my thoughts as he placed his hand on my cheek again. "I've loved you since the moment the stars aligned and brought us together for the first time. You won't lose everyone in your life, Mercy. You have a coven that will walk with you in this life. A coven who loves you. *I* love you."

His words sent my heart racing. He was a man I was both attracted to and drawn to and when he was affectionate, my body trembled at his touch. But he also lied, kidnapped, and held things from me that no one would do to the person they loved. I don't know if the feelings I was having for him were lust or love, but I felt something ... and I hated myself for it.

CHAPTER NINETEEN

We were sitting in Caleb's car, staring at The Danvers City Library entrance.

"Why the library?" I asked him.

Caleb turned to me and back to the library. "There used to be a farm house here, which we owned. The cellar underneath the library was our meeting grounds when our coven joined together. Our village was a few minutes from here. We would meet at a cabin that was built right here to perform spells and train to fight. We couldn't train in the village, as people were starting to become suspicious about the existence of witches. The very first day we learned to fight, it was right here."

My vision. This is where I saw my memories stop during the spell I did with the psychic.

"You mentioned you'd have to draw blood to bind us? Is it going to hurt?"

"Yes, but you'll heal. You heal faster than a werewolf, and they heal pretty damn fast."

I blinked rapidly.

"Yes, they exist," he said casually. "But they aren't a threat to witches. They hate vampires just as much as we do."

"That big wolf I told you about at my house was a werewolf, wasn't it?"

"I believe so, but I don't think he was trying to kill you. Someone had been following you for a while before I approached you at the park. I believe that wolf was trying to protect you that night. They were trying to get you back in the house. Werewolves protect witches."

Wow. That means the person following me these last few weeks was there at my house that night.

"And I sent fisher cats to kill it." I shook my head in remorse.

"Like I said, they heal fast. The only thing that can really bring them down is a silver bullet."

Caleb looked at the time on his phone. "Let's go," he said, halting me from asking any more questions about werewolves and silver bullets.

Once we reached the door, he placed his hand on the handle and then stopped.

"My heart was broken when you died. It destroyed me." He grabbed my hand gently. "If you die again, we all die. We need you to live. We need your strength and your power. But most importantly, *I* need to be able to look into the eyes of the woman I love, every single day of our existence."

I knew he was right. It wasn't about me. It wasn't about what I wanted anymore, it never had been. My life wasn't mine; it belonged to the coven.

"Okay." I looked back at the door we were about to walk through. "I'm scared, but I'm ready."

With a smile on his face, he grabbed my other hand and escorted me inside the library. We took the elevator down into the cellar. Once the doors opened, my eyes were immediately drawn to an engraved pentagram symbol on the floor at the center of the room.

I sat at the center of it as he instructed. He grabbed a few candles from his backpack and placed them around the circle, lighting each one of them.

He grabbed his phone and checked the time. "The spell to make you immortal will take place immediately after your Awakening, which is just a few minutes away. Are you ready?"

"I'm scared."

"I'm right here. Close your eyes."

I did as he instructed.

He spoke in a language I didn't recognize. A gray cloud then formed under my eyes and parted, leaving an image before me, just like I had seen during the spell in the witch shop.

In the scene before me, a woman was cooking something over an iron stove. The room was lit by candlelight. The stove wasn't like anything that we have in modern day. This was my old home.

The woman turned around and looked straight through me. "Mercy, go to your room. I need to speak with Caleb."

I heard a voice behind me and when I turned around, I saw a girl about my current age, with my face, but with red hair and blue eyes.

"Mama, I want to hear what he has to say."

She slammed her hand on the counter, "Go, Mercy. Now."

"No! I am more powerful than you. You cannot make me do anything anymore," she told her mother defiantly.

Caleb was there and was dressed in black slacks with a white shirt under his long coat.

He took a few steps toward the girl and grabbed her hand gently, still facing her mother. "We are doing the ritual tonight. She and the rest of us will become immortal because it's the only way she will be safe. Look what happened to your husband. He could be dead, for all we know. And what about your other daughter, Faith? She needs her sister to protect her. Mercy will be able to protect you both. It is a witch hunt out there, Mary. Why would you not want this for her?"

"Roland lied to you, Caleb. Your father knew more about this prophecy than he shared with us. You will never be safe. If vampires knew she was immortal, knew any of you could not die, they would take you and torture you. They would feed on you over and over again. Not to mention, Mercy's blood will allow them to walk in the light and that will put us all in danger."

"I will protect her. We all will protect her."

Caleb approached Mary. He placed his right hand on her shoulder and squeezed without her fighting back. She was already in a trance before he touched her. He was chanting a spell. She didn't scream and she didn't look like she was in pain. She just stood there with her eyes closed and then collapsed to the floor.

He turned to the girl. "We need to leave as soon as the ritual is done. It will not take long before the vampires know what we have done. Go grab enough clothes for a few days and meet me at the barn. I need to go find the others," he instructed.

After Caleb left the house, she ran upstairs and stuffed a bunch of clothes in a sack. She picked a book from the dresser and a few small blankets and stuffed them into her bag. She then stopped by her bed. Was she having second thoughts? She heard a knock at her door. "Mercy?"

A man walked in, but it wasn't Caleb.

"Dorian, what are you doing here?" A handsome man with dark brown hair and brown eyes ran into the room. He was built like Caleb, strong, tall, but pale and perfect-looking, not rugged, no five-o-clock shadow. It was then I recognized him. He was the man who had been visiting my dreams before all of this happened. He was the one who kissed me under the moonlight night after night, who had suddenly disappeared when Caleb walked back into my life. He wasn't a dream. He, too, was a memory.

He stopped by her bed. "Your mother is right. You cannot allow

Caleb to turn you immortal. They know you are doing the ritual tonight. I came here to warn you. They are on their way. Once the ritual is done, they plan to take all five of you and keep you as slaves. I am not a strong enough vampire to stop them. You saved my life once. Let me save yours."

"I am dead either way." She grabbed his hand and placed it over her heart. "Do you feel that? My heart is steady, I am not afraid. At least if I were immortal, I would be stronger. I could fight back, and you would not have to protect me anymore."

"I would rather you be dead than be tortured by them. At least if you are dead, you will be free," he said.

"We will be apart, either way." She squeezed his hand.

Did she care about this vampire? She was a hunter, well, *I* was a hunter, and I wasn't trying to kill him. Was I not the ruthless vampire hunter I thought I was? These memories weren't like the ones I had after looking at the symbol on my hand. These were more like watching a film, where the others were actual memories coming back. I didn't feel emotion, I just watched. I had to have met this vampire between the age of thirteen and eighteen, as I had no recollection of him from when I did the memory spell.

She grabbed his hand and placed it gently on her cheek, closed her eyes tightly, and took a deep breath in.

He also closed his eyes, but hesitated on pulling her closer to him. It was clear now. He loved her.

"Goodbye, Dorian." She let go of his hands and walked out. I watched as she left the house and looked around.

Dorian moved with lightning speed toward her. "Mercy." Her hair flew up like wind blowing by from the speed of his movements. "You do not have to do this. You can choose death. If the vampires catch you after you become immortal, you will want to die, trust me."

She looked into his eyes and tears fell down her face. They both didn't speak as she closed her eyes tightly. She knew what he was saying was true. She gave him a nod, threw her bag down on the ground, and spun around. "I love you, Dorian."

She fell to her knees and put her hands up in the air as a crowd of angry villagers formed around her carrying ropes and lit torches.

She had chosen death. *I* had chosen death.

Dorian backed away from her, blending in with the crowd, unable to hold back his sobs. It was clear he didn't want her to die, but he must have known it was the only way she'd be free from the endless torture that awaited her.

They couldn't have known Dorian was a vampire because they ignored him as if he were just part of the crowd. They were focused solely on her.

"Witch! Witch!" one called out.

"Hang her now!" another shouted.

Two men, each grabbing a different arm, held on to her tightly and dragged her across a long field. Once they reached the main quarters, there were ropes hanging from a tall tree and people screaming and chanting, "Hang her! Witch!"

I watched as they pulled her on top of the ladder and could now feel their hands on me like it was happening to me. The rope was placed around her neck and I felt it around my own.

I didn't understand why I wasn't using my powers to stop them. True, death was better than being sucked dry for eternity, but I could have at least fled. Fled the ritual, fled this town. I, this girl in front of me, apparently didn't care anymore.

I was now standing on the ladder with the noose around my neck. I was no longer viewing the memory, but I was the girl in the memory. I could smell horse manure and the sweat coming from the man who tied the noose around my neck. I saw Dorian in the crowd and whispered to him, "I love you."

I watched Dorian in the crowd as tears flowed down his cheeks, faster than my beating heart.

"Witch!" they chanted in unison.

"Hang her now!" a man bellowed.

I turned to the man that was about to kick the ladder from underneath me and gave him a warm smile. "Thank you," I whispered.

Everything went black and my eyes popped back open.

I was back in the room with Caleb, in real time. My throat felt like it was closing; like the noose was still choking me. I coughed over and over again, and Caleb held on to me, comforting me. I looked up and his face was pained.

He must have seen my memory.

"Yes, you loved a vampire," he said. "I didn't know he was in your room that night. I didn't know you gave yourself up."

"You saw?"

He ignored my question. "We have to continue. It's almost your Awakening. We have only a minute."

"Why did I see that memory?" I asked.

"I needed to bring you back to the moment you died. I needed to see what your heart truly desired."

"You've had the power all along, didn't you? To bring back my memories?"

"Some memories are better left in the past."

"Where is he, Caleb? Where is Dorian?"

He shook his head. "He attacked us that night and Simon killed him."

My heart crumbled into a million pieces from those words. "Dorian wouldn't do that! I felt the kind of man he was."

"He's a vampire, not a man. And yes, he would kill."

"There are good vampires out there, Caleb. I didn't feel threatened by Dorian."

"We did what we had to do."

Caleb lifted the dagger he was holding and slit the center of my hand. I winced.

"Did you change your mind?"

I shook my head. "No."

"The Awakening will happen in thirty seconds. The blood needs to be drawn to be linked to our coven. It's going to bind you to us. We will become one. This will sting just a bit." He squeezed the skin around the wound and blood dripped down to the center of the circle.

It was happening, and it was happening now. He began chanting while squeezing my hand and he allowed the blood to drip by our feet. He released my hand after he got enough blood. My blood swirled around like a tornado forming from the ground and wrapped around my body. I felt warm, and then hot, like my body was melting, but at the same time, the warmth was comforting and pleasurable. I closed my eyes as it continued to wrap around and swarm my body. A huge burst of energy flooded through my chest and I fell to the ground. The moment didn't last long, but my body felt like it had been running for hours. The blood dissipated all around me and I felt like my whole body was about to explode. It wasn't painful, just overwhelming.

The next moments were much different. Caleb now had his hand on my forehead, speaking words again I didn't understand. Every part of my body was now feeling like it was being ripped apart. I screamed in agony and my nails scraped across the floor. The pain I was experiencing felt like a wave crashing hard against the rocks of a shore. Suddenly, a sharp pain stabbed my stomach. I looked down and Caleb had stabbed me with the dagger right in the gut, but I knew he wasn't trying to kill me; this was part of the ritual. I didn't scream, but the pain was excruciating. He removed the dagger and I healed instantly. I fell to the floor and everything went still.

"It's done." He gently helped me to my feet.

We both stood up from the circle.

"What now?" I asked.

But before he could answer, we heard the elevator ping. When we looked in that direction, Abigail emerged from the shadows.

"Thank you, little nephew." Her grin was sinister, and it made my skin crawl.

"Abigail, what are you—"

Before I could finish my question, fangs protruded from her mouth.

A vampire, of course.

"Step back, Abigail. You're not touching her," Caleb commanded. But his commands meant nothing to her. She wanted my blood.

"I just want a taste."

"Caleb, tell her to put her fangs away before I kill her."

"I only need a few drops. It's not like you would die. I'm just so sick of staying inside during the day. Let me have a taste and I'll be on my way."

She lunged toward me, but in an instant, I felt my body being pulled back through a thick wall, thrusting me forward toward the ground. I got to my feet, looked around the room, and realized I was standing in Lily's kitchen.

CHAPTER TWENTY

Whoa. *Did I just teleport?* I looked up and Joel was standing in the kitchen staring at me wide-eyed.

"Mercy, thank God you're alive," Joel cried.

"That was wild," I said, completely astonished. I glanced at the table behind him, which was covered with candles and burning sage. "What's going on, Joel?"

"Lily was taken," he said, and my stomach instantly twisted in knots. I looked more closely around the kitchen and there was broken glass everywhere. Wine covered the tile from the refrigerator to the hallway.

"After we got your text that you were with Caleb, Lily had a bad feeling, so we came home to grab the items we needed for the locator spell in order to find you. Lily was in the kitchen having a glass of wine to calm her nerves. When I came back in the kitchen, she was gone. I didn't even hear a scream."

"No, this can't be happening. We have to find her," my voice cracked and my hands became unsteady. I felt my powers climb to my fingertips and Joel placed his hands on mine to help calm my nerves.

"Easy, Mercy. I know it's hard to control your powers right now, but take a breath."

I steadied my breathing until I felt the energy subside. "Let's do the locator spell," I suggested, looking over at the candles and sage again on the table.

"I've been trying but it's not working. Something is blocking me. Her car is missing, so there might be a chance that she escaped the intruder and took off, though she would have reached out by now if she were safe." He placed his hands on the table and picked up the sage. "Were you safe? Did Caleb hurt you?"

"No. Caleb did take me but he didn't hurt me. He helped me through my Awakening. I'm immortal now, too."

"Mercy." He was now gripping the sage, crumbling it in his palm.

"I didn't have a choice, Joel."

He shook his head. "We always have a choice."

"Let's focus on Lily right now," I said.

"Do you know who could have done this?" he asked.

"I have an idea, but I don't know who they are. Someone has been following me and they went as far as possessing my friend to hurt me," I explained. "Our guess is that it's a witch who has a personal vendetta against me."

He grabbed Lily's truck keys off the key ring. "We need to find her. Now. Is there any place you can think of that they could have taken her?"

"I don't. I'm sorry."

We were interrupted by my phone ringing. I didn't recognize the number.

"Hello?"

"Hello, Mercy." A low and eerie voice rang on the other end of the line.

"If you hurt her, I swear I will rip your head off."

Laughing on the other end of the line pierced my ears.

"Where did you take her?" I asked, my jaw clenched.

"It really is beautiful out here. I can see why you come out here to think and relax all the time. The moon reflecting off the water, the gorgeous trees, and the peaceful silence ... is simply breathtaking.

"I'm on my way." I hung up.

I banged my fist on the table and looked up at Joel.

"Where is she?" he asked.

"Goddard Park. Let's go."

Joel created a portal that teleported us to Goddard Park. Seconds later, we headed toward the bench where Riley and I had sat the other night when I had met Caleb. I saw Lily's car and spotted her brown hair shimmering in the moonlight.

"Lily, we're here!" I shouted as we both ran toward her.

She didn't move. When we were in front of her, I saw her eyes closed, hands and feet tied, and mouth taped shut. Before I could remove the tape, Joel collapsed behind me. Caleb stood behind him, holding a bloodied rock in his hand.

"Caleb!" I wondered how he had gotten there so fast and why he would knock out my uncle.

I now noticed his eyes were black and his face expressed pure evil. I'd seen that look before in Cami's eyes. He was possessed. Caleb was my stalker's new puppet.

"Whoever you are, get out of him now. If you want to fight, fight in person, and stop using my friends."

I grabbed a large rock from the ground and threw it with every amount of strength I could muster. I hit Caleb's head, barely grazing the side. But it was enough to make him lose his balance and topple over a large branch behind him. I quickly turned around and ran toward the forest. Before I reached the trees, a blaze of flames lit them up in front of me. I halted and swung around. Caleb's hands were raised, but only for an instant, then brought back to his body. Without hesitation, I held up my hands toward the water and Caleb stopped moving. He laughed and threw his head back.

Ignoring his mockery, I used the power from my right hand to pull Joel closer to the bench and used my powers to pull one of the tree branches toward his feet, wrapping them tightly around his ankles and to the bench, keeping him secure. The branches reached for Lily's waist and secured her to the bench. Caleb looked at me curiously, tilting his head, and moved toward me again. I had to act fast. My hands flew up toward the water, and with my mind, I commanded the waves to pull in toward the forest and wipe the flaming trees with water. The water did as I commanded, pulling up onto the park and sweeping away the flames around us. It reached only up to our ankles and I knew it wasn't enough.

Caleb was quick to approach me and pushed my arms to my side, keeping me secure in his grasp.

"Too late," I said calmly as water came crashing down over our heads like a massive tidal wave.

Instantly, Caleb lost his grip on me. I held my breath as the water pulled us under. We were being pulled farther into the cove, but I was able to make my way to the surface as the water started to calm down. Caleb was already on me and grabbed my hair. I spun around and punched him straight in the face. I had never punched anyone before, but it felt liberating.

"Bitch!" he screamed.

I was hoping my punch would slow him down, even for just a moment, so I could escape. I quickly swam to the shore, which took every ounce of energy I had, but before I could reach Joel and Lily, Caleb was behind me, grabbing me by the waist. I kicked my legs in the water frantically, trying to get away. My resistance didn't slow him down as he pulled me out of the water and toward Lily's car.

He laid me down on the passenger seat and we looked out toward the water. My heart was pounding. I didn't know what he was going to do.

"Are you still wearing the necklace?" He looked at my neckline. I gripped the stone. Was Caleb talking to me? Or was he still possessed?

"Caleb?"

"Are you?" he snapped.

"Yes, yes it's on."

"Get out!" Caleb shouted.

He slammed his head back and black smoke came through his eyes and out of the car.

"Are you okay?" Caleb asked, clearly himself again. His eyes were wet and he could barely catch a breath.

"Are you? Holy shit, Caleb. You were possessed. How did you even get here or know where to find us?"

"The portal Joel created was still open, so I hitched a ride here. I saw you on the beach, followed by that smoke entering my body.

"What do we do now?"

Our focus was drawn to the front window of the car and we saw a man standing in front of us. He wore a long black coat, gray top, and black pants. His hair was frosty white and lay right on his shoulders. He looked to be in his twenties. He had no facial hair and his eyes were bright red.

He wasn't a witch, like we thought he could be. He was a vampire. He showed his fangs, hissed and licked his lips. He was clearly evil in its purest form. My heart felt like it was going to explode as my heartbeat pounded hard against my chest. He had handsome features, but when he showed his fangs and hissed, his face transformed into a demon-like creature. He was horrifying.

"What is that?"

Caleb's shook his head. "This isn't good."

"Who or what is that?"

"Remember the demon I told you about that mated with an angel to create the vampire race?"

"That's the demon?!"

"No," he said. "That's their child. The very first vampire to ever exist."

I looked back toward the vampire. "Great." Panic was rising in my chest. "We can't drive away. Joel and Lily are still on the shore. We need to fight him. It's not like he could kill us, right?"

He put his hand on his waist but froze. "The dagger I used during the ritual. It's gone."

"Why do we need that? Aren't wooden stakes how you kill a vampire?"

"There's one weapon that can kill an immortal. It's that dagger."

"Well, the plot thickens. Got to love your secrets, Caleb."

He shook his head. "Son of a bitch."

We looked back at the very pissed-off vampire in front of us. The red-eyed demon held the dagger, tapping it against his leg.

He was so close to us now. He stood in front of the car and laughed.

"My name is Kylan," he said, and my heartbeat picked up at the sound of his voice. "I was hoping to stop the ritual from happening, but you weren't at your home like I thought you'd be." He flashed an evil grin and showed his fangs, his face contorting into a disgusting and vile demon-like creature.

Caleb didn't take his eyes off Kylan. "You're his biggest threat, Mercy. He knows what our mission is. With us alive, he knows we will destroy everything he created, especially with you being back. I wish I had put it all together; that he would be the first one to come after you. He would have known about you, long before the ritual. It was never known to us that he could harness magic." Caleb cursed and slammed his hands on the steering wheel. "I just assumed it was a witch."

"Hey, this isn't your fault. My guess is that he's been hiding for centuries. It could have been anyone, Caleb. Let's fight him. Together." He looked at me and nodded.

We both turned toward Kylan again. We each opened our door and got out of the car, and cautiously walked toward him.

Kylan laughed again. "How precious is this?" He paused and slowly smiled at us. "Look at you two. Back together again after all these years. Too bad you're about to die together. In a way, it's like a tragic love story." His laughter sent chills down my spine.

I had never been so terrified in my entire life. Despite the overwhelming feeling of fear, there was also anger. He was hurting the ones I love. I felt my new powers radiating through my body, and I wasn't leaving this park until this creature was dead.

Kylan took a step closer to us.

"Mercy, run!" I heard Joel's voice.

Lily and Joel were now conscious, breaking off the tree branches that were wrapped around them to keep them from being pulled into the cove.

Kylan was walking toward us. I lifted my hands up and used my energy to shoot the dagger out of his hands and across the parking lot. This infuriated him and he hissed loudly.

Lily and Joel clasped hands together and began to chant a spell. A ring of fire formed around Kylan.

"Really? Fire? Do you know how old I am?" Kylan asked mockingly.

He glared at me and clapped his hands like we'd just concluded the final scene of a play. "I've decided I am going to kill Caleb first, that way, you can watch him die." His head tilted back as he laughed at us, and it made my skin crawl.

"The fire will only last a few more minutes. We need to stand in a circle around the fire ring and be ready when it burns out," Lily said, not acknowledging Kylan's threat. She and Joel were now by our side. The four of us held hands and formed a circle around him.

"I have powers, too, you know," Kylan shouted. "I was the first vampire ever created." He lifted his hands and Joel and Caleb stopped moving. Lily turned to me and her eyes were midnight black.

Oh no.

I held my hands up. "Lily, it's me. Wake up. Fight it."

Lily pulled her hand out to her side and I felt a force of energy radiate inside my body. I realized she was pulling that power from me. The dagger lifted off the ground and flew toward her hand. She clasped her fingers tightly around the dagger and lunged toward me, throwing my backside on the ground. I hit my head on a rock and winced. "Lily, wake up!"

She tried to plunge the dagger into my chest but I fought her with all my strength. I wanted to use my powers but I feared I'd hurt her. My hand flew toward the dagger and I used the force of fire from my fingers to heat up the dagger in her hands. She yelped and released it. I caught the warm end of the blade and tossed it again, behind me. My hands gripped each side of her face and used my energy force to pull the smoke out of her eyes. I shielded my face with my right arm as it exited her body. For a brief moment, I felt it trying to enter my body but my necklace lit up like a Christmas tree, pushing the force away from my body and back into Kylan, who had been standing there, hands in fists the entire time.

He wasn't going to win.

He was now grinning and showing his fangs. For an ancient, all-powerful vampire, he wasn't fighting much. In fact, he really wasn't fighting at all.

"It's over, demon. Let them go." I pulled myself out of my fear, jumped to my feet and helped Lily to hers. She was in a daze.

"It's okay, Lily. You're safe."

Kylan lifted up his right hand and froze Lily like the others. "Fine. I'll find another way," he snarled with gritted teeth.

I held out my wrist. "I'll let you drink my blood. That's the other way. Now that I've gone through my Awakening, my blood will allow you to walk in the light. Don't you want that? Here. Drink."

"I don't want your blood. It isn't as desirable to all of us."

This puzzled me, especially when he laughed. He was so sadistic and now I was alone with him.

The fire burned out around him and he walked over to the dagger on the ground and picked it up. He then did what I wasn't expecting. He walked back over and handed it to me.

I looked at him, confused.

"Take the dagger and plunge it into your heart, or I will gut your aunt right in front of you with it."

I didn't know what to do. The short memories I had of some of the battles I'd fought in my previous life, were brief. I couldn't recall any training that I could use right now, in this moment. How was I supposed to stop the original vampire?

I'm surprised I'm not already dead. Why am I not already dead?

I looked at him with a puzzled expression on my face. "Why are you making me take my own life? Why not kill me yourself?"

He frowned. "It's more poetic."

I looked down at the dagger. This didn't make any sense.

"No," I said, handing him back the dagger, but he wouldn't take it.

"No?" He looked down at the dagger.

"You do it. Make it quick," I ordered, testing my theory.

He frowned again, and his eyes lit up. "Take this dagger and kill yourself with it, witch! You don't want to see what horrible things I will do to your aunt, do you?"

I looked over at Lily and back to him. I was now smiling.

"You can't kill me, can you? Something is not allowing you to do it. And you can't possess me, either because I'm wearing this necklace." I touched the jet stone.

He showed his fangs.

"That's why you used Cami ... because you can't do it. You can't kill any of us. You didn't push her, she jumped to protect me."

This may be easier than I thought.

"Why can't you, though? Why are you not able to kill me?"

He hissed at me like a viper ready to strike. His eyes narrowed, and his fangs appeared again.

"After I ripped my father's head off, my angelic mother put a curse on me."

The sadistic bastard killed his own father?

"But you created vampires. Don't they have to die in order to transition?"

"I only turned one vampire. Her name was Valentina. She was so afraid of what she'd become after I drank from her. After I had explained to her that she would now be a vampire, she took her own life. She didn't realize that was the final step in her transition. Once you die, you're reborn." He laughed.

He was so sick. He loved seeing people in pain ... he thrived on it.

"Her blood lust was stronger than mine. She turned humans into vampires and her creations turned others, and a vampire race had begun. It was like a plague that would never stop spreading."

He laughed again so hard he flung his head back and balled his fists. When he lowered his head again, the red in his eyes had turned black.

This thing was pure evil. He had to die, and now.

CHAPTER TWENTY ONE

"You lose, Kylan. I will not take my life, ever. I will also continue to fight by Caleb's side until every last one of you is dead."

I was making him angrier, but I didn't care. His face started to change. He was so ugly now it was hard to look at him.

"That necklace may keep you from being controlled by me but all I need do is wake Lily or Joel and possess them again and make one of them kill you with this dagger. Then I'll force them to drown themselves. You push that dagger through your heart and I will spare their lives."

"You won't touch them," I warned. I then took the dagger and flung it toward the water as far as I could.

As he dashed for the dagger, I lifted my hands and created a barrier around Caleb, Joel, and Lily. The shield encircled them in a bubble Kylan couldn't penetrate. I chanted:

"Fire from my hands, create this flame.
Make him feel every ounce of pain.
Send this demon straight to hell.
For all I have, I create this spell."

Kylan stopped running. "What's this?" He looked down at his body. "What's happening to me?"

His body was melting, but he wasn't screaming. It just made him angrier. I wasn't pulling this power from Caleb, though. Spirit didn't have to. I was able to control fire and everything around me.

I kept my eyes on Kylan. His flesh was melting from his face to the point that he was no longer recognizable.

"Stop this, you witch!" He barely cried out before his mouth melted off his face and dripped to the ground.

I spotted a fallen branch, ran toward it, yanked it from the ground, and split it in half with my knee. I ran toward Kylan with the sharpest end pointed toward him. He was still standing, but very weak; too weak to fight back. I plunged the piece of wood through his heart. He backhanded me across the face, causing me to fall to the ground. As he screeched, Lily, Caleb, and Joel unfroze and fell to their knees. They all looked up just in time to see Kylan explode into ash.

I bolted toward the water and picked up the dagger. Lily ran toward me and held me tightly. I gave her the biggest hug I had ever given anyone. They were safe.

"We need to hide that dagger," Caleb said while getting to his feet.

"I know a place," Joel mentioned as he lifted both hands up in the air and created a portal. "I'll teleport it there."

He chanted a spell and the dagger zipped through the portal entrance.

"Where did you send it?" I asked.

"Don't tell us where you sent it," Caleb interrupted. "The fewer people that know, the better. There are mind reading witches out there."

"You'll never know," Joel assured us.

"We need to go. As soon as your Awakening happened, every witch felt it, and there are witches that are aligned with vampires.

Your blood is very desirable to them now and their witch allies will lead them to you. We need to hide you until we can put together a plan," Caleb said.

"Where can we go?" I asked.

"Joel, can you teleport us to St. Peter's Cemetery?" Caleb asked while grabbing my hand.

Joel nodded.

"Why take us to a cemetery?" I asked, remembering what happened the last time I was there.

"There's a witch safe house in one of the mausoleums, Mercy," Caleb explained.

It all made sense now. I knew exactly where he was taking us. Seconds later, we were teleported to the St. Peter's Cemetery, where Riley's mother was buried.

"I've been here before." I looked over at the mausoleum across the cemetery. "My friend's mom is buried here. We came here a few weeks ago to pay our respects, and over there, we heard some crazy noises from that mausoleum." I gestured in that direction. "Is that the safe house?"

Caleb nodded. "It used to be a vampire lair. You and I snuck in there once to take out a vampire that was planning to strike a werewolf pack. We owed that pack a favor."

"I think I had a vision about it, but at the time, I thought it was just a dream. Someone threw me down the entryway from behind," I said. Bits and pieces of that vision came back into my mind. I had climbed down some stairs inside a coffin in the mausoleum. Someone had come up behind me and pushed me down.

He smiled. "Yeah, that guy got what was coming."

I looked at him curiously. "That actually happened?"

"It was as if they knew we were coming. They struck you from behind and when you landed, a crowd of angry vampires surrounded you. But don't worry, we were right behind you." He winked at me and grabbed his phone from his pocket.

"I need to call Abigail. She's going to worry about me."

"Don't you dare. She tried to bite me."

"She won't hurt you, Mercy. She's on our side. She couldn't control herself."

"Are those words actually coming out of your mouth?" I couldn't believe he was already dialing her number.

We entered the mausoleum's doors and there was a coffin at the center of it. Joel slid the coffin open and it made the same screeching noise I had heard the day I was there. Someone must have been hiding in here that day. There was a long set of stairs that led under the ground and Joel went in first.

"I need to make sure it's safe first. Come down slowly in about five minutes."

Five minutes later, we entered the lair, and I looked around. It was bigger than I had imagined. There was furniture in every space of the walls; there was even a kitchen and a few bathrooms.

We were down there exploring the space for over an hour when we heard a tap at the door. Abigail walked in. "Do you really think she'll be safe here? It's a vampire lair."

Caleb lit up when he saw her. He really cared about her. "Not anymore, it's not. She'll be safe here. It's been abandoned for a couple centuries." He walked up to her and gave her a long hug then pulled away slightly, while still resting his arms around her shoulders. "We need your help, Abigail," he said.

"Of course you do," she gloated with a side smirk.

Caleb rolled his eyes.

Abigail walked in my direction and sat down on the couch next to me. I wasn't afraid of her anymore, and if I were going to trust her to fight with us from here on out, I wanted to know who she really was.

"Hey," I said gently.

She closed her eyes in annoyance. "Yes, Mercy?"

"Sorry I won't let you drink from me. But you understand, right?" She didn't respond. Instead, she folded her arms like a stubborn child but kept her posture perfectly straight.

After a long pause, she turned toward me. "I'm not being selfish, you know. I can't control my desire for blood. None of us can."

"Who did this to you?"

Her forehead creased. "Who turned me?"

I nodded.

She showed no expression of anger or warmth. She looked away and shifted again in her seat.

"I was thirty-two when I was turned. I was born a witch, as you know, but that all changed after you and your coven began to train. I didn't feel like I belonged there anymore, so I left the village to find my purpose.

"Three years after I left the village, there was word of the witch hunt, and that you had died. I felt like our hope was lost. I didn't belong with the witches anymore, nor was I a powerless human. I didn't belong anywhere. I met a handsome vampire named Lucas Carmichael shortly after Caleb and the rest of your coven fled Salem. At the time, I didn't know he was a vampire. He was so charming, and he treated me like a princess." Abigail smiled wanly. "I wanted so badly to live forever like my nephew, but the Chosen Ones were the only ones allowed to do it. I envied what you had, so when he told me what he was, I was drawn to it. This was my moment to live forever, but in different way."

"So, you asked him to turn you." It wasn't a question.

She nodded. "After he turned me, we moved to a clan in Warwick. I grew to love the vampires there. They were kind to me, and Lucas kept hidden from them the fact that I used to be a witch. Vampires and witches were enemies and always will be, and the punishment for turning a witch was death. We were there for several years."

"How is it that witches today know very little about vampires?" I asked.

"After the Chosen Ones became immortal, vampires feared them, so they hid. If they killed a witch or human, they were discreet about it. They were no longer slaughtering villages and making a scene everywhere they went. It would have only drawn Caleb and the others to them. Witches didn't want mass hysteria, so they didn't write about it or tell anyone about them. A few stories made their way into our history books, but for all witches know today, they were no longer a threat, or they were simply a myth."

I looked up at Caleb, who was leaning against the wall, watching Abigail and me. His arms were folded and his smile was faint. I smiled back to him and turned my attention back to Abigail.

"What took you away from that clan?"

Tears formed in Abigail's eyes. It was weird seeing her so vulnerable. She was so perfect in my eyes. She continued, but her voice became stern. "Lucas brought me a child who introduced herself as Emily. I thought he had adopted the little girl for me. As a vampire, you can't conceive a child and he knew how much I wanted children. I wanted to hold her, hug her, and keep her safe. She was the daughter I never had. I realized what was really going on, when he grabbed her by the hair and shoved her toward me. He wanted me to feed on her. I looked at the girl who had tears in her eyes. She was so frightened. I was beginning to feel emotions that were almost impossible for a vampire to feel. I had no choice but to obey him and drink. As I went to sink my teeth into her neck, I felt a force pull me back, like someone was grabbing on to my head and pulling me from her. I looked down at her neck and saw that she was wearing a black stone necklace. It was a jet stone, the same stone I saw you wear the night you came to my house. As I'm sure you already know, the stone protects witches from demons like me. I didn't realize at the time that this enchanted stone was made by your coven to protect witches from demons, but I knew she was a witch. The stone had been enchanted."

I stared blankly at Abigail as she continued her story.

"This little girl was a victim to something dark and evil. I had asked a vampire to turn me into a monster, just so I could live forever. I was so selfish, I didn't think twice about the lives I would have to sacrifice for my needs. I also knew that this child was a witch, part of who I truly was, and still am inside. I may have lost my powers as a witch when I was turned, but it will always be who I am deep down. I told Lucas I couldn't betray my kind. This, of course, angered him, the fact that I chose a witch over the vampires. He ripped the necklace from her and sunk his teeth into her neck."

CHAPTER TWENTY TWO

"He was going to make me watch her die as my punishment."
Poor Abigail. I can't imagine watching a child being killed in front of me.

Abigail placed her hand over her heart as if she was experiencing chest pain and tears welled in her eyes. "Everything happened so fast after that. I broke the leg off a dining chair and lunged toward him. I don't think anyone there even saw what had happened. I staked him in the heart and killed him. I turned to Emily and she was losing too much blood. I had to save her, so I turned her. After her transition was complete, we fled the clan. A few years later, we met Sherwood. He gave us a place to sleep and he fed us."

"You mean, he let you feed on him," I guessed.

"Not at first. He didn't know we were vampires. We did our best to stomach the human food he served us, but we had to find blood to survive. We would take walks at night and find animals near the forest by his house. It just wasn't the same." She cringed and shook her head. "It's just not natural.

"Over time, Sherwood noticed we weren't getting older, so I had to tell him the truth. Sherwood loved us and accepted us, no matter what. The blood from the animals was weakening us so he let us feed off him from then on. But I knew when to stop so I didn't hurt him. Emily was afraid her old coven would try to find her and destroy her if they found out she was a vampire. So, we changed her name to Desiree."

I gasped, staring at her with wide eyes. "Your house servant?"

"My daughter," she corrected.

"Of course," I said quickly.

Wow. To kill a child for her to come back as the undead must have been awful for her.

I couldn't imagine what those two had gone through and hearing Abigail share the most vulnerable parts of her proved she was one of the strongest women I had ever met. I would be happy to fight beside her.

Lily and Joel had been gathering some snacks and water in the food storage closet for everyone. When they re-entered the room, Abigail shifted in her seat.

I stood up. "I need to keep my friends safe, Caleb. We need to bring them here."

"You're not leaving this lair, Mercy," he ordered.

"No. I'm not saying I have to leave." I turned to my uncle. "Joel, can you teleport them here?" I asked.

"I can. Who do I need to start with and where are they?"

"I can't reach Riley, so it will just have to be Shannon until I can reach him. I'll call her now."

Caleb grunted in the corner and I glared at him. "What is your problem?"

He threw his hands up. "This isn't a fight that will be done by the weekend," Caleb snapped.

"I get that, Caleb. But if we can get as many as we can here, I can cast a spell to protect them somehow. I need them in a place I know they're safe until I can figure out what exactly I'm up against, now that the vampires are aware of my Awakening."

He stormed off. I didn't understand why he was being such a jerk.

I stood and put my hand on Abigail's shoulder. "Thank you for telling me."

She didn't look up, didn't acknowledge me anymore, and I accepted that. It probably took a lot for her to open up that part of her life to me.

Caleb cursed in the distance.

"What is wrong with you?" I asked as I approached him.

"I don't like this. I can't protect you while worrying about the safety of your friends."

"They will be safe here. I can't fight when I am worrying about *their* safety."

He walked up to me, slid his hand around my neck as if he had a right to touch me, and pulled me in.

"You're the most important person in my life." He gently pressed his forehead to mine. My heart rate picked up at his touch, but I couldn't allow myself to feel this right now. I had to focus.

I placed my hands on his chest and pushed him away slightly, giving us some distance, and backed away from him. I pulled my phone from my pocket and he shook his head.

Shannon's phone rang once before she picked up. "Oh my God, Mercy! Are you okay?"

"Yes and no. Look, Shannon, I don't have a lot time to explain, but—"

"Riley found me," she interrupted. "After what happened to Jeff. He told me that he saw you being taken against your will by Caleb. I swear to God if he touched you ..."

"No, I'm okay. Caleb didn't hurt me. I need to explain something that you may want to be sitting down for." I suddenly felt nervous to tell her.

"Is this about you being a witch and how vampires are after you?" she asked bluntly.

I caught my breath. "How did you ..."

"After you were kidnapped, Riley told me everything. I didn't believe him at first, but then Jeff tracked me down. He figured I knew. He was freaking out about what you did for him. Is this a joke?"

I shook my head, even though she couldn't see me. "No, it's not a joke. This is real, Shannon, and it's not over. I need to get you here, and now. There are vampires out there that are going to hurt the ones I love in order to get to me. I can't let what happened to Cami, happen to you."

"Cami was hurt by a vampire? Wow. This is unreal, Mercy. I knew you didn't mean what you said. I'm sorry I didn't understand at the time," she cried.

"Stop, Shannon, all of this is my fault. I can't fix what happened to her but I can save you and Riley. I don't want to risk them finding you on your travels up here, so my uncle is going to teleport you here." I waited for a gasp to come from the other end, but it was much louder.

"Teleport?!" she screamed.

I had to pull the phone away from my ear until she calmed down. After she stopped screaming on the other end of the line, I instructed her to pack a bag and stay on her couch until we brought her here. She agreed, but a part of me felt she doubted the whole story of witches and vampires. I knew this kind of news wasn't the easiest to believe. Even though I couldn't physically show her my powers, I knew being pulled through the walls of her home and into a vortex would be proof enough.

I tried Riley's phone again.

Please, Riley, pick up. Pick up.

His phone rang a fourth time before the answering machine picked up.

Dammit.

~

We spent the next hour trying to devise a plan on how to draw out the ones that would seek me out, before they found me first. The last thing we needed was to be snuck up on. We needed to keep my friends down here while we scoped out some of the most prominent vampire clans in Salem. The problem was, they'd smell me a mile away. We needed to find a spell to mask my scent.

Shannon texted me to say she was on the couch and was ready. I wasn't sure how long we'd be at the safe house. These vampires weren't going away after this weekend but keeping her close until we saw what we were up against was the smartest and safest move. Riley still wasn't answering his phone, but I left a message about where to find us.

My next call was to the hospital where Cami was admitted. I spoke with a nurse who informed me that she had woken up an hour ago but wasn't speaking to anyone at the hospital, not even her doctor.

She's at least alive.

"Cami's awake," I told everyone, shutting my phone down. Lily's whole face lit up.

"The spell must have been broken when Kylan died," Joel explained.

"She's still not safe. Can you bring her here, too?" I asked.

Joel shook his head. "No, I won't do that. Cami has been through enough. Pulling someone through a portal takes a lot out of the person. I don't think it would be the best thing for her health, to put her through that," he explained.

My heart was pained at this news. I knew it was best not to put her body through any more stress, but not having her here, where I knew she'd be safe, worried me.

Joel lowered his eyes and caught my gaze again. "The only spell I can think of is a cloaking spell. The nurses won't see her but if they touch anywhere on the bed, they'll feel her," he said.

"Do it, then. It's the best chance she has," I said optimistically.

"But, Mercy, I can only do it for one person because it's linked to me. We will need to lock Shannon down here and hope no one penetrates the locks."

I nodded. "Let's do it." I looked up at the clock and saw that it was half past midnight.

Joel was working on the cloaking spell from the kitchen and building the portal through which he'd teleport Shannon.

They'll be safe soon.

Shannon stepped into the lair and looked around. Her hair had been whipped around from her journey and she was shaking. Her eyes shot wide open, and her jaw dropped as she looked around. The amount of supernatural overload was probably overwhelming her in that moment.

"This ... is ... crazy, Mercy." Shannon shivered as she took in the room around her. "That was insane."

Abigail was standing in the doorway to the kitchen, looking into the dining area where we sat.

"Why is she staring at me like that?" Shannon asked, her voice trembling. "I mean, is she ... she's not a witch, right? She's something else?"

"Oh, for crying out loud. I'm not going to bite you."

Shannon squealed and backed up. "Stop looking at me like that."

"If I were going to eat you, I would have done it before you could ask that question. I don't kill humans."

Shannon gulped, but kept her eyes on Abigail. Caleb was in the lair's training room, pounding out his frustration on a boxing bag, while Lily and Joel were working on making Cami invisible for the time being.

Lily broke from Joel and welcomed Shannon with a hug. "It's a lot to take in, I know. You'll be safe here," she promised.

I turned to Shannon when Lily released their hug. "Did you ever get a hold of Riley?" I asked her.

Shannon nodded. "Yes. Finally. He's picking up his new friend, Amber, and then they'll just drive here."

"Amber? Did we go to school with her?"

"No. I met her tonight after the football game. She's the girl who found him after the wolf attack."

I checked my phone one last time to see if Riley had tried calling before turning back to Shannon. "Okay, we'll start without him and I'll fill him in when he gets here. Well, if he gets here."

I caught her up on the events from the evening in more detail than I had over the phone. I explained the ritual, my mission, my sole purpose for even being in this world, and the powers Spirit gave me. Finally, I explained my immortality and my destiny to protect humans. Surprisingly, she expressed her acceptance of the new me and her desire to help in any way. She was shocked, yes, but it was now her reality, too.

Caleb emerged from the training room after pouting in there the last hour. Sweat was dripping from his neck, and he was breathing heavily. He hastily interrupted us. "We need Mercy to start training. She needs to learn to fight."

"Mercy? Fight? This should be interesting," Shannon snickered under her breath and I playfully rolled my eyes at her.

I walked into the training room. It was quieter than the rest of the lair. It had a padded floor and weapons stretched all the way up to the ceiling. Caleb explained that witches created this place after they took the lair over. The adult witches would bring their children here to train them, just in case they needed to fight witches that were into dark magic. Back then, vampires weren't a threat to witches anymore, but not all covens were allies.

A radio hung on the wall by the door. Caleb walked over to it, turned on a rock station, but lowered the volume.

"You get reception way down here?" I asked.

"It's the only station that will come in somewhat clearly." He softly laughed. "I hate fighting in silence." He pulled a hairband from his pocket and wrapped it around his hair, pulling it into a man-bun. He then removed his T-shirt, revealing a black tank top. His muscles were hitting the material just right, showing off the definition of his abs through the thin cotton material.

Damn.

He walked up to me, pulling out another rubber band from his pocket. "Here, tie up your hair. It's about to get really hot in here." His sideways smile and not-so-subliminal sexual reference made me blush.

I tied up my hair and joined him in at the center of the room. He held up his palms. "My hands are your target. Don't hold back."

CHAPTER TWENTY THREE

Over the next couple of hours, he showed me kicks, jabs, upper cuts, sweeping, punches, and strikes. "It would be much easier if my memories of how to fight came back. Can't you just do what you did during my ritual and show me everything from my past?"

"Even if they did, you'll remember the moves, but you still need to practice. This new body of yours is weak and skinny. We need you to be able to side-kick your opponent and actually knock them down."

"Okay, I get it. I'm a frail little girl that no one in their right mind should trust to save them. Caleb, I can just use my magic."

He shook his head. "I wish that were enough." He walked up to me and placed his index finger under my chin, lifting it up slightly. "Your physical strength has heightened since the Awakening. You just have to learn to use it."

"Alright. Just, go easy on me."

"Not a chance," he said with a huge grin on his face. He came up from behind me and put his arm around my neck in a choke hold. "Now, try to pry my arm away." The heat from his breath tickled the back of my head, weakening me at my knees. "I'm your enemy right now, Mercy. Do what I showed you."

I gulped and closed my eyes. As he had shown me before, I

grabbed his arm, pulling it down from my neck, stepped to the right, and elbowed him in the chest, hard. He winced and backed up slightly. Now taking his arm, I twisted it behind him, holding it firmly. "Don't hold back, Caleb."

His face crunched and blood rushed to his face. "I'm not, Mercy. That was all you. You can let go now." He grunted and released a deep breath he had been holding in.

I released him and he straightened back up. "Now kick me," he commanded, and I did just that.

I shifted my body slightly to the left and side-kicked him, but he grabbed my foot and twisted it, but it twisted my entire body and I fell to the floor. He was on me before I could get back to my feet and pressed his chest against mine, pinning me down. He forcefully grabbed my wrists and pinned them above my head. My heart rate picked up again. As he glared into my eyes as if he were devouring me, I wiggled out of his grasp, placed my hands on his chest, and blasted him off me. He flew so high up that he slammed into the ceiling above me and then plummeted to the ground. This time I didn't apologize. I knew he was okay.

"You see? I can just use my magic."

He proudly smiled at me and came to his feet. He leaned down and kissed me on the forehead. "Let's get some water."

We both took a swig of water and got back to the mat. Before we could start again, we heard a commotion coming from the main living space of the lair.

"Stay here," he barked, but I wasn't having it.

"No way. I'm coming with you."

He shook his head and cursed under his breath again.

We walked in and saw the others on their feet.

"We heard the coffin lid opening. Someone is here," Lily said.

Caleb's phone rang. He answered it but didn't take his eyes off the entrance. I heard another male voice on the end of the line talking and Caleb nodding his head.

"Okay, got it. Thank you for the warning." He hung up. "That was my father, Roland."

"Your father?" I remembered him telling me his father had been turned centuries ago.

"A vampire was at the cemetery when we arrived here and went back and reported it to her clan. They're going to strike soon."

"So, your father doesn't have allegiance with his clan?" I asked, but he didn't answer. "Caleb is your father on our side or not?"

He looked back to me. "Yes and no. He's faithful to his clan, but he was sworn to protect the Chosen Ones, and he will. Right now, he's on our side, but if we come after his clan, he won't be able to protect us."

Joel ran up and interrupted us. "Someone is coming down the ladder. Get ready."

The reality of this new life, that was now mine, had hit me. My chest tightened as I heard the sound of someone coming down the ladder. I stood in front of Shannon, ready to fight for her life. Ready to fight for all our lives. We stood on guard as we heard a knock at the door.

"Open the door, Mercy. It's me."

We all sighed with relief. It was Riley!

Riley entered, and we came in for a warm hug. He was safe. A girl I didn't recognize stood behind him.

"You must be Amber," I said, while releasing Riley's hold.

She smiled and held out her hand. "Nice to meet you, Mercy."

I looked at her hand but didn't shake it. "Nice to meet you, too." I knew I was being rude, but this was weird timing, her coming into our lives. Why would he bring her here?

I punched Riley on the arm and he barely flinched. "Really, Mercy? What the hell?"

"I've been worried, Riley. Where have you been? I've been trying to call you for hours." I was now shouting. "And then I have to tell you we're in trouble on your voicemail! Then you bring a stranger here. No offense, Amber, but there is a lot going on right now, and you're a stranger to us," I said plainly, waiting for her comeback, but she didn't look upset.

A low growl came from Abigail, which halted Amber, who looked as if she were going to say something.

"Abigail, what is it?" I asked her. Abigail's fangs instantly appeared.

"Abigail, stop that! Riley is my friend, and this is his friend, Amber. Put those away!" I commanded, as if I was chastising an untrained dog.

"That's okay," Amber said. "It's her natural instinct to try to kill me."

"No, Amber. She doesn't kill humans," I told her.

I looked back at Abigail who still was growling at Amber. "Abigail, seriously. Put your fangs away."

Abigail looked at me fiercely. "You didn't mention you were friends with werewolves."

Wait, what?

I looked back to Amber. "You're a werewolf?"

Amber took a step in my direction. "I was the one you almost hit with your car when you crashed that morning. The same one who saw Kylan outside your home that night you sleepwalked outside your front door. He had a witch with him that was using their powers to draw you out through your dreams. I tried to keep you inside your house, but you called the fisher cats on me."

Another unsettling feeling hit me. There were witches that could control my dreams?

"Oh no, Amber. I'm so sorry. I didn't know what was happening," I apologized.

She took another step toward me. "I wanted to transform into my human form and tell you. I didn't think me talking to you with my mind would have helped you relax any better. It was safer that the vampire following you always saw me as a wolf."

"Well he's dead now. I killed him tonight," I said, full of pride.

She smiled. "My pack showed up to the lake right as he turned to dust."

"Your pack?"

She lowered her head, as if she were ashamed of something.

"About that ..." She looked over at Riley who had been standing against the wall, watching us converse.

"I needed help, Mercy. My pack has been missing for months. I've been following these vampires since your mom tried to kill you, trying to protect you from Kylan and others like him. Kylan had been following you for months, sometimes right outside your backyard."

We were right. It was him this whole time, following me in the shadows.

"We're about to face some very dangerous vampires that will be coming after you," she explained. "Werewolves have always been aware of the prophecy that the Chosen Ones would come to Earth and protect us. We want to win this fight just as much as you do. Without my pack, I'm nothing. I needed help."

"Why do you keep saying that?" I looked over at Riley again. "Amber, what did you do?" Panic rose in my voice.

There was a moment of silence before Shannon walked toward Riley and looked into his eyes.

"Abigail," Shannon called to Caleb's aunt, her eyes stayed on Riley. "Why did you say wolves, and not wolf?"

Abigail sighed deeply. "Your friend Riley is one of them."

I was stunned silent for a moment, then looked deep into Riley's eyes.

He can't be. Not Riley.

"Mercy, it's okay. I want this," he tried to explain, but I backed up.

"No, no. You didn't ask for this. She did this against your will."

Amber shook her head like she couldn't understand why I was so upset.

"I feel stronger than ever, Mercy. It's the most amazing feeling in the world. Now I can help protect you."

"Oh, Riley. It's not your job to protect me."

I grabbed Riley's hands and Caleb, who I hadn't noticed until now, was by my side. He stiffened up when Riley's fingers touched mine. I looked over at Lily and Joel while still holding Riley's hands. "What do we do now?"

Joel straightened up. "Well, now that we have werewolves on our side, this will be a much easier fight."

I shook my head. "No. Absolutely not. Riley is not fighting."

Joel sighed. "Mercy, we are going to need all the help we can get. He's strong now. You need to trust him. That's why Amber turned him in the first place. With werewolves on our side, we have a fighting chance."

"He's right, Mercy. I can handle this. Let me help." Riley squeezed my hand gently. "This isn't your decision. Besides, werewolves can heal just like a vampire can. It's going to take a lot to kill me."

"Like a silver bullet?"

"Yes, Mercy. Like a silver bullet. If the vampires aren't expecting us to be there, they are highly unlikely to have any on hand, ready to shoot," he explained, but it didn't make me feel any better.

I had faced a vampire before and I had taken one down, but I'd had powers to do it. Riley may be able to quickly heal, but he could still die. I hated this. I knew we needed help from werewolves, but at what expense? Would I so willingly put my friends in danger in order for them to protect me? It wasn't Caleb, Riley, or Lily, or even my human friends they wanted, it was me. I also knew I wouldn't be able to stop Riley from helping me. He loved me and would take a bullet for me if he needed to. Even a silver one.

I sighed and squeezed his warm hand, feeling the need to pull away from his touch, as the heat pierced my skin. The fact that I could touch him again without anxiety pulling through my chest, made my heart full. "Okay," I hesitantly agreed.

Amber and Riley's attention snapped toward the front door and it startled us.

"What is it?" I asked.

"Someone is outside. They're about a hundred yards from the tomb. I can hear them," Amber said.

"And smell them." Riley sniffed the air. "It's not human."

"Huh, it's not a vampire, either." Amber sniffed the air and looked at Riley. "I've never smelled anything like it."

Great! What else is out there?

"We need to leave now," Lily joined in. Joel and Caleb grabbed their weapons and headed toward the ladder that led out.

We ushered Shannon into a secured vault. We gave her the code to unlock the door and some food and water. There was a landline inside the vault and she was instructed to call us if anything or anyone breached the walls.

Shannon turned around toward me before she entered the vault. "I can't believe this is happening. My friend is in a coma, caused by a vampire possession, and my other best friends are a witch and a werewolf. This is something that happens in movies, Mercy. Not real life."

I gave her a warm hug and held her for a few seconds. "Nothing is going to happen to you. I swear it," I said. "I'll be back for you once we know it's safe."

But could I really promise that? Three weeks ago, I was a semi-normal human who was oblivious to the supernatural world. I didn't know I was a reincarnated witch. I didn't know vampires and werewolves roamed the streets and I most certainty didn't know that I was the weapon that could bring it all to an end. Fear engulfed every part of my being and no promise to Shannon was going to make her feel better. How could it? Our plan was stupid. We had no idea where these vampires lived. They could smell me, not the other way around. How was I going to fish them out? We were just going to run and "play it by ear".

Abigail stayed behind to stand guard until whatever was lurking outside lost interest and left.

"Let's go," I told Caleb, but he was already by my side, gripping my shirt and pulling me back toward him.

"Not that way," he told Lily and Joel, who stopped moving toward the stairs. "There is another way out. There is a tunnel that leads to the other side of Park Ave. It will spill us over to Harrington's Antique shop. The entry is at a secret passage way behind the library shelf in the study. Let's go."

Caleb told us we'd have to steal a car once we reached the exit of the tunnel. We wouldn't last long on foot. Joel's portals stayed open for ten to fifteen minutes after they were open. It would be too risky to let whatever was out there follow us through the portal and catch us off guard.

Once we reached the end of the tunnel, we spotted a gray SUV across from a bar on the other side of the antique shop. It was right after four in the morning, so someone must have had too much to drink and gotten another ride home.

Lily placed her hand on top of the car, closed her eyes, and chanted. The car unlocked and started up.

"I really didn't think that would work. It's been a while." She smiled with pride. She'd definitely missed using her magic.

We pulled out onto the road and headed back to the marina. We needed to get whatever was following us away from the lair so Shannon would be safe.

"We don't even have a plan," I huffed, feeling completely incompetent to fight anything.

Caleb poked his head out of the window, searching for our new enemy. "The plan is to kill it, whatever it is," he said.

"I'm ready," Joel said as Lily sped up.

"Can you still smell it?" Amber asked Riley.

He sniffed the air. "I smell something different. Not what I smelled before at the house. It smells like a bird this time and it's close."

Lily sped up to about ninety miles per hour. I knew we had to get as far away as we could, because we really didn't know what we were up against. Whatever was following us was foreign to this newly-formed wolf pack.

We drove for almost a half hour, heading west, unsure of where we were going. We just needed to keep driving till we lost whatever it was that was tailing us.

"Behind us, guys," Lily said while looking in the rearview mirror. We heard a high-pitched whistle above us, as a large bird came crashing into the front window and Lily slammed on the brakes. Glass shattered all around us. She quickly pulled over on the side of the road and turned toward the back seat. "We can't out-drive it. We need to fight."

CHAPTER TWENTY FOUR

I looked through the shattered windshield and saw an abnormally large eagle flying upward. Seconds later, it circled around and started a nosedive toward us. This time, it crashed through the window on Riley's side and began pecking at his arm. Riley didn't flinch, but it sure pissed him off. Joel moved to the side as Riley and Amber jumped out.

Before they could react, the eagle grabbed hold of my hoodie through the broken window. I screamed for it to stop and hit it several times on the head. Caleb grabbed my right arm from the front seat while Riley grabbed the bird's tail and pulled it off of me. The bird flew back up in the air as Riley released him.

A loud growl rumbled from behind the car. I turned around to see Amber in her wolf form and Riley taking off his shirt and pants. He bent down on all fours and his back protruded upward, showing his spine, pushing up against his skin. Hair follicles pushed through his skin and his face pulled forward, forming a long muzzle. The transition into his wolf form was a lot faster than I'd seen in movies. He didn't seem to be in any pain, which gave me some relief.

Whoa.

There was so much going on; I didn't even notice Caleb, Joel, and Lily were now outside of the car. Caleb threw a ball of flames at the large bird as it came back down and Lily used her powers to blast the flame faster in its path, but it dodged the flame and flew back at the car, gripping me tightly again, this time digging its claws into my shoulder.

"Son of a bitch!" I screamed. I lifted my hands up and blasted my energy force toward the bird, hoping it would injure it enough to back off. The green energy knocked the bird on the ground, with its feather's scattering around the street. It was on its feet within minutes again. Joel shouted from behind the car. "I think I know what this thing is, guys."

"Shapeshifter?" I heard Lily shout before I was pulled through the window, my legs being cut open by the shattered glass. The eagle pulled me higher and higher up into the air. I grabbed the bird's legs and pulled its talons apart, causing it to screech and finally release me. I landed hard on the ground and Lily and Caleb were immediately by my side.

"So that wasn't just a very angry bird?" I asked, panic rising in my voice.

"That creature will be back. We have to move, now!" Joel shouted.

"Joel, I think you should teleport us somewhere, if you have the strength. If he follows us, so be it. We at least know what to look for if it hitches a ride." Lily panted from exhaustion.

I looked at Lily then at Caleb, who was looking up at the sky with his hands open, forming a new ball of fire on his palm, waiting for it to come back down.

This is never going to end.

I shook my head. "No, we can't keep doing this. I can't risk your lives. It's after me, not you guys." I knew there would never be an end to running until we knew what and who would come for me. If I allowed myself to be taken by them, my friends would be safe, and I could maybe talk to them. I could perhaps find out their plan, and work from the inside.

"Get in the car, Mercy," Caleb snapped.

I shook my head again. "No, Caleb. You can't save me this way. We're just running. Where are we going to go?" I asked, throwing my hands up. "How many lives will be lost from you trying to protect me? I can't lose the people I love." I looked over at Joel and Lily's direction, who were now walking toward me. Caleb's hands were clenched into fists and Riley and Amber were circling the car in their wolf form.

I took a few steps back and held up my hands, creating a force that pushed Lily and Joel back.

"Mercy, stop! What are you doing?" Lily cried, not able to move her legs forward anymore.

"Dammit, Mercy. Get back in the car!" Caleb was now shouting, his face bright red from anger. "Now!"

"Don't do this, Mercy. Please," Joel pleaded.

"I won't let any of you get hurt because of me," I cried.

I ran into the street and let the energy force drop. I could hear their feet pounding against the pavement as they chased after me. But I didn't look back. I didn't stop. The sound of heavy wings flapping echoed across the sky. Second later, I felt the eagle's talons dig into my shoulder and it pulled me up into the air.

The truth was, I wasn't really giving up. I would still fight, but the farther this creature was from my friends, the better chance they had at survival.

I tried to communicate with the bird verbally, but it wasn't responding to me. I tried to speak to it telepathically, but nothing. It was neither animal nor a human, so I wasn't sure if it took a different set of abilities for me to reach it. I lifted my hands to use my levitating power on its talons to pry them from my skin to ease the pain, but remembered I was now very high up, and that it would suck if I fell. I closed my eyes, trying not to think of the pain. I knew I would be able to heal myself, but this pain was almost unbearable. It only felt like a few minutes had passed before I looked down and could see the Salem Witch Museum. We descended to the ground and the eagle set me down gently.

The eagle lowered its head between its two front claws and its body suddenly grew larger and larger. The feathers seemed to fold into themselves while human skin formed around them. There now stood a man in human form in front of me.

He was very tall, maybe six foot seven, with an athletic body, dark brown hair that grew past his shoulders, and a long goatee. A large tattoo in black ink spread across his chest, over his shoulders and wrapped around his muscular arms. His eyes were a light shade of brown and his skin was dark tan. He was huge. I mean ... huge. I had never been so close to someone so well-built and intimidating. His other tattoos were all of animals: an eagle, a bear, a wolf, and a lion, all on his chest alone.

He walked over to a nearby trashcan and lifted out a plastic bag. He pulled out an outfit from the bag and proceeded to get dressed. I thought about using my powers on him, but whoever sent him would send another and another. The only way to fight these evil forces was to start from the inside, from wherever he was taking me.

The man walked over to me and I noticed he held a metal bracelet in his hand. He grabbed my arm gently and fastened the bracelet around my wrist. I tried to pry it off, but it required a key.

"What is this?" I tried again to pull the bracelet off, but it was still no use. "What did you do to me? Take this off."

"Sorry, Akasha. That bracelet prevents you from using your powers." He spoke in a distinctly Hawaiian accent.

"Akasha? My name is Mercy." I fiddled with the bracelet again. "Dammit."

I can't fight them without my powers.

"Akasha is what vampires call you. It means Spirit, or, Fifth Element." He frowned. "What would you rather me call you?" He was oddly polite.

"Mercy, please."

"Okay then, Mercy. We walk from here."

He grabbed my arm and escorted me toward a nearby park.

"Where are you taking me? What do you want from me?" I asked, but he stayed silent. I moved around, hoping he would ease up on his grip, but he didn't. "What's your name?" I asked, hoping a simple question would get him talking.

"My name is Noah. I was sent here to bring you to the master." He gestured ahead. "We aren't far from where I'm taking you."

Noah clearly wasn't much of a talker. I tried to engage in conversation as we walked, but he wouldn't respond. I even tried to make a few jokes to ease the tension as fear was rushing through my body, but he didn't crack a smile. We walked for about thirty minutes before we arrived at a tall black gate in front of a beautiful, very dark, and gothic mansion.

I was exhausted and all I wanted to do was lie down, even if it was in a strange and dangerous place. Noah rang the bell on the outside of the gate and announced his name and that he had Akasha with him. The gates opened slowly, and Noah gently dragged me through the entrance and along the long driveway. Once the gate closed behind us, Noah released my arm. I now saw the rest of the house that was apparently going to be my prison.

The house was made of gray stone with detailed carvings on every inch of its structure. There were three stories and each story had several windows facing the front. The balconies featured large stone gargoyles that seemed to glare down at me. My heart skipped a beat as I took in the view above me. This wasn't just a house, but a dwelling where something dark and evil resided. I feared what was ahead of me, but I wasn't going down without a fight.

Entering the house, my eyes were drawn to the front room that was filled with three black couches and a machine of some sort sitting in the center of the room. It was a clear case with tubes that protruded from the inside and into small glass vials surrounding the machine.

"What is that?" I looked at Noah.

He, as expected, remained silent.

"Noah, I'm not your enemy."

He looked at me expressionless. "You really want to know?"

I nodded.

"If one of the humans the vampires drink from tries to run away, the punishment is death. They are then placed in that glass chamber, hooked up to those pipes, and drained until all their blood is emptied into those vials. Blood is never wasted here, so if we are going to kill them, we might as well take the blood while it's fresh and pumping through their veins. They store the blood in a cooler downstairs."

My jaw fell open, and my stomach was in knots again.

"You see, Mercy. I *am* your enemy."

What was I thinking, sacrificing myself? I'm going to be their next meal.

I didn't see any residents but could hear laughter coming from closed double doors down the hall. Noah was staring at the doors in front of us, but we didn't enter. I walked ahead toward the doors, not wanting to wait any longer to find out what they were going to do to me. Noah grabbed my hair and pulled me back.

"Ouch! Quit it!" I was so exhausted from the last twenty-four hours, I almost didn't care at that point what happened to me.

Almost.

"Honestly, Noah. I just want to lie down. I may have powers, but I am also in a human body and humans sleep. Do you sleep?"

No response.

That didn't shut me up. "Noah, you don't seem all that scary to me. You don't belong here anymore than I do. You're not like them," I said, and waited for a reaction.

Noah started to give a sideways smirk, then quickly became serious again as he heard a door open. It caught us both off-guard. Another guy, a little shorter than Caleb, was walking toward us. He was handsome with a strong jaw line and ashy brown, medium length hair, slicked back over the top of his head. His eyes were hazel, and they looked right through me as he approached. He looked to be in his late twenties. He was wearing all black with a black trench coat that reached to the floor. Once he was about three feet in front of us, Noah got down on one knee and bowed to him.

"Master, I brought her to you unharmed, just as you asked. The wounds on her shoulders have healed, which further proves that this is Akasha. She has indeed gone through her Awakening and is now immortal." Noah quickly stood up.

I looked straight into the man's eyes. He walked around me slowly, touching each part of my body. He ran his fingers through my hair and lightly touched my neck with his cold fingertips. A chill ran up my spine. He then put his hands on my shoulders and rubbed where Noah's claws had been embedded. He traced the markings that were almost, but not quite, healed. They were simply red marks now. He stood in front of me again and placed his hands under my chin and lifted it up. He slowly traced his fingers down my cheek and to my lips and smiled.

"You are so beautiful. I heard Spirit was perfect, but I had no idea he or she would be *this* perfect." He smiled again. "And now you belong to me."

No, you creepy, yet good looking vampire, I do not!

"What do you want from me?" I finally asked.

"My name is Maurice, and I am the master of this house."

He glanced at Noah who was now right in front of him. "You may go now, Noah. I will get your report tomorrow. You served me well."

"Mahalo, Master." Noah proceeded down the hallway and through the double doors.

Maurice turned back to face me. "Akasha!"

He paused as I shook my head. "You can call me Mercy," I mumbled under shaky breath.

This man really scared me.

He laughed. "Mercy no longer exists." His smile that followed sent a wave of unwelcome goosebumps over my skin.

I wasn't a praying person, but I said a silent prayer that I'd find a way to get the bracelet off, so I could show them how powerful I really was.

"The famous witch I have been learning about for years is finally born again and made immortal. Not only immortal, but she now carries the blood that will make me stronger, faster, and a day walker." He smiled again, sending another wave of fear through my entire body. "You're my own personal blood witch."

"You do know I have the power to use all five elements at once, don't you? You will be dead before sunrise," I threatened nervously, realizing it was just an empty threat. I had no idea what I had gotten myself into.

"Not with that bracelet on your wrist you won't." He laughed to himself. He was right, I was defenseless with the bracelet on my wrist, but I wasn't going to let him believe I was feeling defeated.

"You don't own me," I quickly snapped and took a step back.

The corners of his mouth turned up into an evil grin and he grabbed my hand gently. "Come with me, Akasha."

"Oh, I can't wait," I said sarcastically

We walked toward the double doors. A few times, I put on the brakes as Maurice tightened up his grip as he led me to the doors at the end of the hall. He opened the doors to a room filled with possibly twenty to thirty vampires.

Everyone was lying on beds and couches, some on the floors, and some holding humans that had been bitten, and there was blood everywhere. My stomach churned, and bile rose in my throat. The smell of copper flooded my senses.

A few clapped as we entered and a few hissed at me. It was mostly the females that gave me the unwelcome invitation. I knew I was immortal, but I honestly feared for my life. Vampires didn't even exist in my world until I had met Abigail, and the stupid bracelet on my wrist was keeping me from protecting myself. Just because I was immortal didn't mean I couldn't feel pain.

"Please don't hurt me, Maurice. I have done nothing to you." I turned toward him.

He raised the side of his mouth, chuckled to himself slightly, and showed his fangs. "How about this, Akasha. I will promise not to kill you, but I can't promise I won't hurt you." His response sent a wave of laughter throughout the room. His words and the sound of their laughter terrified me to the core. The unimaginable horror that awaited me hit me like a ton of bricks. In that moment, hope left me, and the sight before me, of blood, torture, and evil, became my reality. I was a toy for them, a walking blood bank, and there wasn't anything I could do to stop them.

CHAPTER TWENTY FIVE

"**Q**uiet, everyone!" Maurice shouted. Everyone came to an abrupt halt. Maurice smiled and gestured toward me. "I'd like to introduce the newest member in our home. The Fifth Element, or as we refer to her, Akasha." Everyone cheered and shouted, but slowly quieted once Maurice raised his hand up. Once the room was completely silent again, he continued. "The ritual was performed and now her blood will change our kind forever. Every vampire clan in the world plans to seek her out, but we got to her first. She is ours."

There was another round of applause, even from some of the humans.

"She will make us stronger, faster, and allow us to finally walk in the light." I heard whispers from those around us, discussing my presence there, and a low growl came from Maurice. I sensed he was getting irritated with the interruptions.

"Silence!" he yelled, and the room instantly became quiet again. "I plan to have her blood to myself for a while, and then I will share her with those who prove themselves worthy."

They applauded him again.

A woman from the opposite side of the room with an Irish accent called over. "Can I 'ave a taste, Maurice?" Then a roar of talking and pleading filled the room.

"Silence!" Maurice screamed again, much louder this time, while raising one of his hands up for the second time. Quiet followed and several vampires looked away in shame.

"Forgive me, Master. I should not 'ave asked," the Irish woman apologized, lowering her head.

Maurice walked toward the back of the room until he was in front of her. He placed his hands on her chin and lifted her lips to his. He kissed her softly, then took both his hands and placed them on each side of her temples. Maurice twisted her head so fast it completely disconnected from her body and the rest of her turned to ash. He tossed the head against the wall and it crumbled to powder.

I couldn't hold in the scream that left me. I quickly turned around and ran for the door. I knew I wasn't going to get far, but I couldn't stop my feet from moving as far away from the sight of a decapitated head as I could. Two vampires quickly jumped in front of the door to prevent me from escaping. Without looking up, I tried to move around them, but was grabbed by my shoulders and swung around to face the room again, their hands now gripping tightly around my arms, forcing me to face Maurice. Maurice walked back over to me.

"Let that be a lesson to you all. You will never ask for her blood and you will never address me unless you have permission. Let's pretend we are all in a classroom and start raising our hands. The only topic that is forbidden is Akasha." Maurice smiled to himself.

He was now next to me and I cowered while leaning back into the chest of the other vampire that was holding me in place. I didn't even care that this other vampire was just as evil as Maurice. I just had to find comfort in someone. The closer Maurice got to me, the closer I clung up to the body holding me in place. I turned my head and buried my face into their chest, not looking up. Maurice placed his hand gently on my shoulder, trying to turn me around.

"Dorian, you can let go of her now."

My gaze snapped up toward the vampire holding me.

I felt his hands slowly releasing my shoulders while I stared into the eyes of a familiar face. It was Dorian. *My* Dorian.

Oh. My. God!

My mind suddenly blacked out into another time. I was in the barn training with Caleb.

"You're forbidden to see each other. You cannot fight the vampires while you are distracted by love, if it's even love," Roland told us. Caleb had his arms folded and he stomped off and out of the barn.

"Is there no other way?" I asked. We're just supposed to be alone for the rest of our lives? It's not fair, Roland."

"You were never supposed to come here and fall in love, Mercy. You're a soldier."

"We promise we won't let it distract us from the mission."

"Whenever the rest of the coven is in danger, the first one he saves is you. You can't fight this way. The answer is no. I have your mother's support on this. We need to continue our training."

I shook my head and turned around. I couldn't look at him anymore. I ran out of the barn, trying to find Caleb, but he was gone. I turned to run toward a small hill by the farm and heard shouting coming from a clearing.

"Caleb!" I shouted.

When I reached the top of the field, it wasn't Caleb who I saw.

"Kill her Dorian. Do it," a woman commanded him, but he shook his head.

"Look at her, she's terrified. Please don't make me do this," he pleaded. He helped a young woman to her feet, who was shaking profusely. This only infuriated the woman that was giving him orders.

"You're worthless. I should have never turned you." She leaned down and picked up a branch from the floor. I saw her snap the end, creating a sharper point. She then turned to Dorian, who was still helping the girl to her feet.

No!

I remembered the memory like it was yesterday. I ran as fast as I could while reaching into the holster around my waist and pulled out my stake. I leaped toward the woman and plunged the stake into her heart. She exploded into ash in front me. I turned to Dorian whose eyes were wide and terrified. "She was going to kill you," I said, grabbing him by the hand. I didn't fear him, and yes, he was a stranger, but his kind eyes spoke to me like no other had ever done.

"Mercy, back away," Roland shouted from the opposite end of the clearing.

I looked back to Dorian and took a step closer to him. "Run."

My memory then sped up, taking me through an entire year of memories with Dorian. I saw our love grow and the feelings of trying to fight it. I watched every memory become a part of myself again, as if it had never left me. I watched us together, until the moment my neck was snapped by a rope.

My eyes popped back open.

I looked up at Dorian, standing in front of me in this room filled with blood sucking vampires, wondering if he even remembered me. There was no emotion in his eyes. He wasn't ripping the head off Maurice in my honor. He was acting like I was a stranger. He was acting like ... one of them.

Why hadn't Dorian come for me? Simon had never killed him like Caleb told me, so Caleb had lied. Why hadn't Dorian come for me after I came back into this life? Did he know who I was?

Dorian caught my eyes and shook his head discreetly, and he

adjusted his shirt as if he were uncomfortable with me looking at him now. He only focused on Maurice.

Was that expression a warning to not let him know that we knew each other?

Dorian had the same face, but his hair was shorter than it was in my memories, and even from my visions that came through my dreams. He had messy, medium-length hair that stood taller on the top than the sides and had the beautiful light brown eyes that I remembered from my dreams, which I now knew to be memories. He wore all black and a long red scarf around his neck. Dorian's eyes met mine again and his face went still.

Maurice grabbed my hand gently and we headed out of the room. I looked back at Dorian as we exited and gave him a pleading look.

I tried to reach him with my mind.

"Dorian, if you can hear this, please help me."

I wasn't sure with the magic bracelet on my wrist, he could read my thoughts, but I hoped he could.

Maurice brought me up a long spiral staircase near the front foyer. We stopped on the second floor and headed toward the very last room at the end of the hall. We walked into a large room with a canopy bed. The canopy posts had beautiful carvings all the way up and a red, silk cloth was draped over it, creating a cover to the bed. The king bed was covered in black bedding with several throw pillows. There was a vanity on the corner of the room with a gaudy vintage mirror. The closet was open and there were dresses and heels that aligned the walls. Were they expecting me? Or was this room always made for women coming and going?

"This will be your room, Akasha. We treat our blood donors with hospitality here. However, if you disobey me, you will spend the night in the dungeon below. I want you to feel at home here, but you are still my slave. You have your own shower and your closet is filled with clothes your size that Kyoko, my right hand, picked out for you once we learned that Spirit was a woman. You are expected to be bathed daily, perfect hygiene, hair and makeup done, but not overly done. You will always be presentable in my presence. If you need anything, you press the speaker button here and Kyoko will come to your aid."

"So those you drink from, they are donors? Not kept here against their will?"

He laughed. "Most of them came here of their own free will."

That thought alone was so disturbing. Why would anyone sacrifice themselves to be fed on and imprisoned like this?

"Get some sleep and Kyoko will be at your door in the morning with breakfast." He leaned in and kissed me on the forehead. Was I just a blood supplier for him? Or did he expect us to have a weird master-slave relationship? Because that was never going to happen!

I stayed stiff as a board as his lips touched my skin. My heartbeat picked up, and I had to control my breathing, as my heartbeat pounded hard against my chest. I was afraid those lips would work their way toward my neck. Aside from his good looks and his charming stature, he was a killer, a sadistic predator who was keeping me against my will and had plans to feed on me.

"Goodnight, Akasha. I will see you in the morning." Maurice shut and locked the door behind me. I had so many thoughts and fears running through my mind, but in that moment, I needed to sleep. I couldn't remember the last time I was this tired. I looked at the clock and it was now seven in the morning.

I crawled into bed and drifted off.

I awoke to a knock at the door. Assuming it was room service, I rolled over and looked at the clock on the nightstand. It was two in the afternoon.

"Come in," I called through the door.

I heard the door unlock and a tiny Japanese girl entered the room with a serving tray on top of a rolling cart.

"Good morning, Akasha. I have your breakfast," she announced. "My name is Kyoko, I hope you like the clothes I bought for you." She opened the armoire next to the bed. "You should wear this black strapless dress today, with your hair down, and that red clip in your hair." She pointed to the dresser. "He will like that," she said as she walked back toward the door. "It is very nice to meet you."

"I don't care what he likes," I snapped.

"Oh, but you must. It is far better that way. He will make the process less painful if he likes you."

"Process? Like when he drinks from me?" Was she a slave, too, or completely delusional?

"It only hurts if you fight it." She winked and then shut the door behind her before I could get in another word.

I thought about my friends and family. Were they safe? There was a part of me that wanted them to bust down the door and help me take down these evil creatures, but that would just put them in danger. I needed to find out as much information as I could about this clan, find a way to escape, and then use that information to bring them down with the help of my coven. We weren't thinking when we ran. We had no plan on what to do because we didn't know what we were up against. I now knew, and I truly believed with my coven, Lily, Joel, and the werewolf pack, we could take them out.

My thoughts turned to Dorian. Would he come with me when I escaped from here? Was he loyal to this clan? Or was I kidding myself into thinking we could have what we had all those years ago?

After I ate and showered, I opened the armoire to pick out my outfit for the day. I decided against the black dress and chose a blue spaghetti strap tank with black jeans. I pulled my hair up and put on some light makeup. I didn't want to be punished for not looking somewhat presentable. Sitting on the edge of the bed, I waited for someone to come get me. After an hour, nobody came, so I walked up to the speaker and pressed the button.

"Hello? Is anyone there?"

"Hello, Akasha. It's Kyoko. I will come get you now."

Ten minutes later, I heard the door unlock. Kyoko opened the door and shook her head. "I said black dress, but I guess that will do. Let's go."

We headed downstairs and I had to ask her the question that had been lingering in my mind since I'd met her. "How do you know how it feels? Are you human? Were you turned?"

"I was a human two hundred and fifty-three years ago. I was brought here, just like you. I still remember the pain I felt when I was drained. If I laid still, it didn't hurt, but when I struggled, I wanted to rip my own heart out. He took so much blood from me, he could either kill me or turn me. So, my vampire turned me."

"*Your* vampire?" I asked.

"Every human the clan takes is assigned a vampire. He or she is yours, and you are theirs. The older vampires have seniority on the witches brought in. The blood from a witch tastes so much better than a human, but the blood from you, Akasha, well, it's been prophesied to be the best. That is why our master wants you all to himself. I own a witch now, and each day I drink from him, I feel stronger and faster."

This cannot be my reality now. I have got to get out of here.

We heard laughter coming from two men in the dining area. I recognized Maurice's laughter, but I wasn't quite sure about the other one. We entered the dining area and Maurice was sitting next to a man I hadn't expected to see—Roland. He was strikingly handsome, just like his son.

Suddenly, I was having another memory.

Here I go again.

I was back in the training room at the age of thirteen with Caleb, Leah, Simon, and Ezra. This was the same memory the psychic had brought me out of. Roland reached out his hand to bring me to my feet after I had just turned my first vampire to ash. He brought me in for a hug. "I'm so proud of you," he said.

I felt a sting to my face. "Wake up." Maurice was standing over me.

Did he just slap me?

"Where did you go just now?" He demanded that I answer him.

"I don't know. I just spaced out. I think I need coffee," I lied.

He laughed and glanced over at Roland, who wasn't laughing. "Weak and pathetic humans. Kyoko, make her some coffee," Maurice barked.

I sat down directly across the table from Roland as Kyoko rushed to the kitchen. I looked into his eyes and my heart ached a little. Roland had stepped in as a father figure when my own father went missing and now he was a part of a malicious clan that was keeping me against my will.

"Akasha, this is Roland," Maurice said.

Roland held out his hand but I didn't take it.

"I know who he is," I snapped. I felt rage build up in me. He was a traitor. He helped raise me, and he was sitting here as one of my captors.

"You remember?" he asked, tilting his head to the right.

"Do you, though?" I asked. "Remember me?"

Roland may have warned us about the clan coming after me, but he wasn't trying to rescue me. He was next to Maurice and all he had to do was stand up and snap his neck and help me escape. No, he wasn't my ally. He was Maurice's best friend, and this was a game to them.

"Of course I know who you are, Mercy. I trained you when you were a little girl."

Maurice glared at Roland.

"Relax, Maurice. I helped raised this girl. She's Mercy to me," Roland told him and then tilted his head at me again. "Has my son been training you?"

"He's teaching me well. When was the last time you saw him?" I said, taunting him.

"Akasha, hold your tongue!" Kyoko snapped at me while placing my coffee on the table.

"It's okay, Kyoko. She has every right to be angry with me," Roland said.

I didn't know whose side Roland was on. What were his intentions? Was he going to help me or not?

"Mercy, I'm on your side." A voice echoed in my mind.

Roland looked at me and nodded while Maurice was asking Kyoko to call in Dorian and Noah.

Apparently, we shared the power of telepathy. I was amazed he was able to still use those powers after being turned into a vampire. I wondered if it was just this gift alone he could use, or if there were more abilities he still had in this form. I also realized when I projected my words to Dorian, he may have heard me after all. The bracelet wasn't blocking that power. Caleb told me I had to only focus on speaking with my mind to one person and that I couldn't lose focus of the person I wanted to hear me, or others would be able to listen in.

Roland looked away from me and focused his eyes on Maurice. What was he planning?

"You have to let me go, Maurice. You can't just keep me here." I needed to distract Maurice somehow.

"Sure I can. I own you now, remember?" His voice was eerily calm.

"Let me go!" This time I was in Maurice's face. He now looked annoyed with me.

"*Easy, Mercy. Just let me drink from you.*" Roland told me telepathically.

"*You are out of your mind. Get out of my head if you are going to say stupid things like that!*" I projected to Roland's mind.

Roland spoke out loud. "Mercy, your blood is very much desired here in this clan. Maurice has allowed me, and only me, to drink from you, other than himself. That was the deal for me giving your location."

"*You gave him our location!? Jerk!*" I projected.

"You're not touching me." This time I spoke out loud. I glared at them both.

Maurice laughed again. "Isn't she adorable? She's so defiant." His demeanor quickly changed as his pale face grew stern. "I never break a promise and I won't start with Roland. He gets the first drink."

"*You sold me out.*"

"*Trust me, Mercy.*"

"Well, I don't," I said out loud. Oops. I was getting confused on what was in my head or from my lips.

"What was that?" Maurice asked, puzzled.

"I ... I said don't touch me."

"You still don't get it," Maurice snapped.

"I get that you're a sadistic bastard who I can't wait to kill someday." I waited for a slap to come, but all he did was laugh.

I understood now that Roland wasn't warning us earlier at the safe house, he was fishing us out of there, so I could get caught. He had a plan but I wasn't sure if it was in my favor or against it.

"Just think, moments from now, I will get to enjoy rays of sunlight on my face. It's the only thing I hate about being a vampire." He smiled at Maurice and they laughed in unison. "But I guess that won't be a problem anymore, now will it, Mercy?" Roland smiled at me.

There was a moment of silence while two very attractive blood suckers grinned at me. A shiver ran down my spine. I was more disgusted than afraid.

Roland stood up and walked toward me slowly. Maurice was holding both my shoulders with a firm grip.

"Don't do this, please," I pleaded. I was not ready to be fed upon. This was a complete violation.

At that moment, Dorian entered the kitchen to inform Maurice that everything was set for tonight. Maurice smiled and quietly asked Dorian to call for Noah. Dorian left the room and quickly glanced over at me, then continued out the door.

Roland was now by my side and placed his hands on my shoulders. Every muscle in my body tensed the instant he touched me.

"What's going on?" Roland asked Noah, who was now standing at the door.

Noah didn't say a word. After a few more minutes, Dorian walked back in. Dorian looked at me nervously and drew in a deep breath while Noah approached Maurice. This time I kept my eyes on Dorian. What was happening?

Maurice placed his hand on Noah's shoulder. "What is happening with her coven? You said this morning is wasn't just witches. I want your full report."

Noah straightened up. "I counted three other witches, a human, a vampire, and two werewolves. The witches and werewolves were the ones that were helping her escape. I didn't see the other elements there."

Maurice crunched his nose. "Werewolves, Akasha? Really? You have werewolves as friends?"

"At least they would never turn their backs on their own kind." I glared up at Roland, who just shook his head at me.

"Once the werewolves could smell me, they headed toward the secret tunnel they think we don't know about. I don't know what they're up to, but after Mercy—" he stopped and cleared his throat. "After Akasha had surrendered herself, they went back to the safe house. They didn't sleep all night. They are planning something."

"You surrendered yourself?" Maurice paused. "Interesting."

I didn't speak.

"Maurice, I'd like to test out the daylight while we still have it. Can I drink from her now?"

"Yes, of course. A deal is a deal." He gestured toward me.

"Go ahead. Drink," he instructed casually, as if I were just an appetizer he was serving a guest.

"You mean right now?" I cried

No! This can't be happening right now.

Roland smiled. "Just relax. It won't hurt you if you relax."

So I've heard.

Roland pulled my ponytail to the side and leaned down toward my neck. I felt the heat from his mouth crawl up to my ears. The only thing going through my head was why in the hell was I just sitting here. Without thinking of the consequences, I pushed the chair back, toppling Roland over and onto the ground, and ran for the door. It took only one second before Noah had his hands on my shoulders and yanked me back, placing me back into the chair.

Son of a bitch!

"Noah, allow me." Dorian walked up to me and Noah backed

away. He pulled my ponytail once again to the side and gently tilted my head. His touch was soft and gentle. I instantly relaxed, not looking up at Dorian or even acknowledging him. With my eyes closed tightly, I took a deep breath.

Roland walked up behind me while Dorian continued to hold me still and I felt sharp fangs pierce my skin.

CHAPTER TWENTY SIX

I t didn't hurt like I had anticipated. It was almost pleasurable. My body relaxed. Everything about me had enhanced since the ritual. As the blood was being drained, I could feel it pulling through my veins, and every now and then, my wounds tried to heal around his fangs. A relief hit me that I could still heal, even with my powers being blocked by this bracelet. The drinking only lasted less than a minute before Roland released me. After he let me go, I felt a slight moment of euphoria and lost my balance, falling toward the floor.

Dorian caught me and I landed gently in his arms. I looked up at him. There was a feeling of peace and hurt at the same time. This was never Dorian's desire. He hated that he had to feed on humans to survive. He never once wanted to be a vampire from the moment he was turned.

"I don't want to waste any more time, Maurice." Roland licked his lips and then wiped the remaining blood off from his chin with a towel from the kitchen. "It was nice doing business with you." They didn't shake hands and he didn't say goodbye to me. He quickly turned around and headed toward the front door. I wasn't a person to any of them. I was property, and this was a vampire testing out the merchandise. The vampires in the room shielded themselves from the light outside as the door opened and closed.

Dorian helped me to my feet and Kyoko went to grab a wet rag.

My wounds were now healed, but I was covered in my own blood. Dorian softly dabbed the blood from around my neck with another kitchen towel. Maurice grabbed the rag from Dorian's hand and signaled him to move away from me.

"Burn this rag, Kyoko, then escort Akasha to her room to shower off her blood. Noah, mop the floor until every drop of her blood is cleaned up."

My strength was now coming back to me and I stood straight. I looked over toward Dorian, but he wouldn't even look at me. Was he ashamed he hadn't helped me? Could he help me? I didn't want him to risk his life for me, but I needed to know if I really had someone on my side.

Maurice turned to exit the room, but I needed him to know I was going to be the worst prisoner he had ever had. I wasn't afraid, I was angry.

"What are you waiting for? Just drink from me, you demon."

His laugher came out over the top as if mocking my defiance. "The first time I take a drink from you, my love, I do it as part of a ceremony. It will bind you to me. I will feed from you and then you feed from me."

The hell I will!

"I have a loyal witch that performs a ritual while I drink from you. This is what binds us. I will always know where you are and what you're feeling, and you will feel the same way about me. You'll want me to feed on you. Tonight, we do the ritual. And to make sure you don't fight it, Noah is bringing me some leverage."

I didn't like the sound of this. "What kind of leverage?" I gulped.

"A little human friend seems like a nice appetizer for me, don't you think?"

No. This can't be happening.

"Maurice, I swear I will kill you if you touch her." My hands balled into fists. "I promise you, I will make you ash before dawn, and I don't need my magic to do it."

"I would love a little sparring match with you." His sinister laugh made my blood run cold.

My fingers dug deep into my palms.

He leaned in toward me, no longer grinning. "I'm going to bathe you in her blood."

Without thinking, I leaped out of my chair and lunged toward Maurice. I knew I may not have my super witch powers with the bracelet on, but I knew a little bit of kickboxing from the short training sessions I'd had with Caleb, Lily, and Joel. I used all the strength I could to knock him to the ground. Once we stumbled to the floor, I kicked him in the face, causing him to fall back. He was up on his feet before I could kick him again. His hands were on my wrist, twisting it back, and his other arm wrapped around my neck in a chokehold. He used his knee to slam into the back of my legs, bringing my knees to the ground. My knee caps slammed against the hard tile floor and I winced.

"You are no match for me, witch. I am eight hundred years old." He let go of me and left me in my defeat. While my body repaired itself, Maurice stomped out and signaled for Noah and Kyoko to follow, but Dorian was still standing by the wall. He slowly walked toward me.

"Here," Dorian said as he reached out his hand.

"Um, thanks." I grabbed his hand and stood to my feet.

He let go of my hand and turned to walk out, but I grabbed his hand again. He turned around but wouldn't look up at me.

"Look at me, Dorian."

His head tilted up, only slightly, and he looked ashamed.

"You know who I am, don't you?"

"You're Akasha." He wiggled his hand from mine, releasing my hold.

"Why are you pretending to not know who I am? I've seen visions of my life before this one. My face is the same."

"What are you talking about?" he asked.

His tortured stare that followed was familiar. It was the same way he had looked at me when the crowd took me away to be hanged. The look that told me he loved me but couldn't stop what was to come. He tried to turn away, but I grabbed his wrist, halting him.

"Stop. Please, talk to me," I begged. He turned back around but didn't speak. "Dorian."

"We can't talk about it. Not here. There are cameras everywhere," he whispered.

I looked up toward the ceiling near the corner of the room. He was right, we were being watched.

Kyoko entered the room again. I quickly dropped Dorian's wrist.

"I'm supposed to brief you on today's activities and the rules of the house, but we need to get you cleaned up. I can still smell your blood from across the house." She looked over at Dorian. "What are you still doing in here? Get back to your assignment."

Dorian didn't look at me again. He turned to Kyoko and bowed his head. "Of course. Sorry. I was just making sure we didn't miss any blood on the floor." He turned around and walked out.

I sat down at the table next to the kitchen and my eyes spotted a painting on a wall I hadn't noticed before. The painting was of a demon whose skin was dark red. He was naked with black, bat-like feathered wings. He looked like the devil I had always imagined. He was holding a beautiful woman in his arms who was wearing a long white dress. The demon's mouth was open, showing vampire fangs, and he was staring down at her neck. He didn't look anything like the vampires I had met. These vampires here were all beautiful, pale, and humanlike. The creature in the picture looked like something straight out of the depths of hell. I looked away from the painting as Kyoko walked toward me and placed a knitted bag on the kitchen table.

"Do you like that painting?" She gestured toward it.

"It's terrifying," I admitted.

Kyoko sat down and stared at the painting with me. "His name was Misha. The devil himself had a plan for him that would forever change this world. He was only a baby when he was sent here and a couple living in a small village that couldn't have children took him in as their own. As terrifying as he looked, they loved him.

"His parents tried to feed him milk from the mother's breast and food from their farm, but he threw everything up. One night, they found him feeding off their sheep. It was the only thing he wanted. Blood. His instincts took him to blood, unknowing and unforgiving as those instincts were. It was the only way for him to survive. He also grew at an abnormal rate. Within a year, he was a grown man."

As disturbing as this story was, the more I knew about vampires and their original creator, the easier it would be for me to fight them. Kylan may have been the first vampire, but this was the demon that created him in the first place. I wanted to know more, so I stared at her intently. My gesture caused her to perk up, eager to share more of their dark history.

"Then one night," she continued, "while Misha was sleeping, he had a dream. In the dream, the devil appeared and told him why he was sent here in the first place. He told him he was to create an army and humans were to be their slaves and food supply. Misha was filled with so much evil, he obeyed without question, the devil's instructions. It was Misha who gave us the name 'vampire'. He only had to feed a human his blood and then kill them. Once they woke, they had to feed on human blood. After that, the transition would be complete, or so he thought."

She continued, "The vampires he turned had transformed into what Misha looked like, not like the vampires you see today. Their outsides were red, demonic, and frightening to humans. He knew this would be a problem. It's much easier to charm someone to be their victim when their appearance was beautiful and approachable. He also had no control over these vampires. They were like rabid beasts with no intellect or humanity to control. He knew he had no choice but to kill all that he had created and start over."

She stood up and walked toward the painting. My eyes followed her around the table and she stopped in front of it, placing her hand on the white dress the angel wore. "It was then that Misha had another dream, where the devil told him there would be an angel sent to Earth to stop him." She removed her hand from the painting and looked over at me. "The devil told him to destroy her.

"One day, he was tracking the forest by his house when he saw this beautiful woman. Her name was Tatyana."

Kylan's mother.

"She was wearing all white and her hair was golden blonde that fell straight down to her waistline. Misha was taken aback by her elegant beauty and was determined to have her, even though he knew this was the angel the devil had told him to kill."

She joined me back at the table. "We don't know if Tatyana was forced to lie with him, or if she wanted to be with him, but together they made a child. He wasn't going to destroy the angel that was sent to stop him, but he would use her to create his army.

"They created a half-breed. His son would be the one to create the vampires. He'd make them demonic on the inside, like himself, but beautiful on the outside, like Tatyana. They would also have half of their humanity inside of them, but they lost their soul." Kyoko smiled. "Tatyana named her son Kylan."

I cringed at the sound of his name.

"When Kylan was born, Tatyana was relieved to see that he did not look like Misha; red and demonic. He was beautiful and perfect, just like her. Kylan was not able to eat human food, either, so Misha fed him only blood. Misha would fetch the blood first, then serve it to Kylan because he didn't have fangs yet to drain victims. Tatyana was hoping he wasn't a blood drinker, like Misha. Kylan took a few years to grow into a man, but then, like Misha, he stopped growing.

"One day Tatyana was cooking supper when Kylan came into the room covered in blood. As she looked closer, she could see Kylan's fangs were out and in his hand was the head of his father."

It was such an unsettling thought. He was so evil, that he would so willingly cut off the head of his own father.

Kyoko's face hardened. "Tatyana knew Misha would not be the first victim. It was in that moment she placed an angelic curse on Kylan. According to the curse, he could never take a life with his own hands. Unfortunately for her, he had the gift to possess others and make them do what he wanted. He turned one vampire, who finished her transition on her own by taking her own life, and his persuasion allowed him to spread the vampire race throughout the world."

"Angelic curse? Wouldn't that be a gift? To make someone not able to kill another person?"

She shook her head, appearing annoyed by my question. "Tatyana abandoned her son after what he had done. She could no longer stop him once the vampires started to spread all over the world. The vampire race grew so big, witches and werewolves were no longer able to defend themselves.

"Tatyana knew she needed help after she had failed, so she

created the Chosen Ones. She chose five families in Salem that carried incredible gifts. She told them they would each conceive a special witch that would come to Earth to help stop what she started. Fortunately for us, we stopped her plan by capturing the key element needed to make that happen. You." She smiled, full of pride. "I hope you meet Kylan someday, Akasha. He is a great man."

Oh, I met him, all right.

CHAPTER TWENTY SEVEN

"Why did Kylan kill his father?"

She smirked. "I love this part of the story. Kylan was hiding in the stables when he saw the devil from the underworld demanding Misha kill his wife. The devil knew she would try to stop their plan. Kylan could never kill his own mother, even if she tried to turn on him."

Caleb never told me this much in detail about the origin of what brought us here. I was strangely thankful Kyoko was telling me about their origin. I was now discovering more of who I was and how important I was to this world.

"This painting was created by Kylan himself, to remind him of where he came from." Kyoko looked at the clock. "I'd better start explaining the rules of the house. But first ..." Kyoko grabbed a silver bracelet from the knitted bag. She walked over to me and exchanged it for the one I already had around my wrist and snapped it tightly shut, before removing the first one. "There you go. It fits perfectly."

"Why did you change them?"

"Like the other one, it blocks your magic. But this one also has a mechanism that will send an electric current through your body, completely paralyzing you, should you try to escape. There's a cord that runs around the property boundaries that will trigger it if you pass over it." She giggled to herself like a little child. "It's like one of those invisible fences humans use for their dogs."

I grabbed my wrist and lowered my head as tears started to form again. I wanted to be brave. I was angry and there was no doubt I would fight for my life at every possible chance. But in this moment of exhaustion and fear that they'd hurt the ones I loved, I could not stop the tears that now rolled down my face.

"Please don't cry." She placed her hand on my back. "Maurice is very charming, and he will be gentle with you when he drinks your blood." Kyoko scooted closer to me. "There are only a few rules here in our home. Obey your master. Don't try to run. And you need to eat plenty of human food so you have your strength. The only light sources you will have are the lamps and candles that are always on during the day and night. The shutters are locked shut during the day hours, so we will provide you with vitamin D supplements."

I lifted my head. "You don't sleep in coffins during the day?" I asked innocently.

She laughed. "No, we don't need to sleep. We just make sure all the light from outside is shielded from entering the home during the day."

I looked at her with pitiful eyes. "I would rather die!"

"I know. I have been in your shoes before, remember?"

I kept my voice to a near whisper. "Then take this off my wrist. I will spare your life. Help me escape," I begged.

Kyoko's face became angry and she snapped. "Don't confuse my kindness with me liking you. You are still a witch and I am a vampire. You are only food to me." She sat up, straightened her clothes, and grabbed her bag. "Follow me upstairs. You look terrible."

I was a bit taken back by how quickly her tone had changed. I thought maybe because of how kind she had been with me, she was someone I could trust, but I was wrong. Perhaps Dorian was the same as her. Showing me a little bit of kindness, but still loyal to the clan.

Back in my room, I pulled my hair over my right shoulder and traced my fingers over where Roland had bitten me. I felt completely violated.

Tonight, I was going to be drained of blood and fear was starting to take over me. I also knew it was only a matter of time before Shannon would be brought in by these creatures as "leverage".

I decided to make the most out of the day and learn everything I could about this clan, hoping it would in some way help me.

I spoke with several humans and witch slaves that were held here against their will. When the vampires were not feeding on their slaves or donors, they allowed them to wander the house and interact with each other. They had books for them to read, several different televisions, and plenty of food to keep them healthy. They had specific foods for the prisoners to eat. They said the healthier the food, the better the blood tasted. There was always a vampire watching them. The vampire that was assigned to me when Maurice was away was his brother Colin.

Colin was turned after he noticed Maurice wasn't aging. Maurice knew he would have to leave his family and wanted company along the way, so he had turned his own brother. Colin looked to be in his mid-twenties, and wasn't as good looking as Maurice, but still had some of the same features. He didn't have a lot of power with the clan. Maurice was the master and Colin abided by his brother's commands. The way Colin watched me was unnerving.

It was a relief for me to meet other witches and learn about the different powers they held. They all talked about having the same kind of experience I had with being bitten. If you relaxed, it didn't hurt. Fortunately for me, I was able to regain my strength right away after being bitten, unlike the rest.

While I was talking to the other witches, I gravitated toward Sarah. She was one of the first witches I talked to. We had to do our best to speak quietly whenever we were around Colin or Sarah's vampire, Troy. Vampires had a strong sense of hearing and they were always nearby.

It was hard, though, to keep quiet when Sarah first mentioned her power.

"You can do what?!" I lowered my voice by the last word as Sarah gave me a sharp look. Troy wasn't far away, and we didn't want him interfering.

"I can make people see things that aren't there or manipulate someone's face to look like someone else," she explained patiently. I hadn't even heard of powers like that before. "If I could use magic right now, I could make you see flowers blooming in my hands or trees growing in through the windows, or I could make Troy look like Steve Buscemi."

I giggled at the mental image, sneaking a glance at Troy out of the corner of my eye.

Right as I looked, a vampire on the other side of the room called out for Troy, waving him over and out of the hall. Finally! We can speak normally again!

"That's so interesting."

"You should ask around later, hear what some of the others can do. Like, you see April over there?" Sarah pointed at a blonde woman, slim and a bit older than both of us. "She can manipulate light and camouflage her body to blend in with her surroundings. And Rachel can make plants grow a lot faster, better. I don't remember what else she can do, but she used to have a lovely flower shop before ... before she was brought here."

My excitement dulled again as I looked at the witch Sarah was talking about and imagined how much happier her life had been back then.

"She must miss it," I muttered, watching Rachel stare out a window.

"Everyone misses their old lives," Sarah shrugged. "Everyone lost something."

Something in her tone struck me.

"What about you?" I asked before I could stop myself.

Dammit, that was not appropriate.

Sarah sighed, looking away.

"Almost everyone, then."

What does that mean? Did she lose her family?

As if she could see the questions on my face, she frowned and continued, "Things aren't black and white, Mercy. Maybe my life wasn't exactly ideal before I was taken here. It's not like I wanted this, but I'd been running from someone else, and my vampire's not a bad one." I had no idea how to respond. Her vampire wasn't a bad one?

April hesitated as she walked past, on her way out the door.

"You okay, hun?" she checked, looking concerned at the expression on Sarah's face. Not angry, but certainly not happy.

"Yeah, I'm fine," Sarah reassured her. "Have you met Mercy yet?"

I let Sarah change the subject and smiled at April.

"Not yet!" she chirped. "Heard about you, of course. I could feel your Awakening yesterday. We all did. Like there was this sudden strength we'd been missing our entire lives, you know?"

Actually, I didn't know that. I knew my Awakening would make a difference, but for everyone to feel it immediately? I hadn't really expected it.

April, Sarah, and I talked together for a while longer. They told me about how they and the other witches had heard stories about the Chosen Ones coming to Earth centuries ago, but they didn't know our purpose, nor did they know that vampires existed until they were caught and brought here. When I described my ability to communicate with animals and how I was able to use all five elements at the same time, they were fascinated, and a few other witches joined the conversation.

We shared stories about our pasts. Some witches, like Rachel, used their powers in everyday life to support themselves, while some had been taught to hide their powers completely. Making one mistake in the wrong place, in front of the wrong people, had brought them to this house. In return, I told them how my mother had taken my powers hostage my whole life and that when we all escaped from this place, they'd be able to use that link to my powers from there on out.

At the mention of escaping, a few witches froze. Sarah tilted her head to the left, and I noticed the vampire standing off to the side, staring right at me. He heard. He totally heard.

A chill ran down my spine as our gazes locked. He tucked a strand of long, raven hair behind one ear and held one finger to his lips, as if telling me to be quieter before going on his way. Was he going to pretend he hadn't heard anything?

"That's Silas," Sarah murmured. "You're lucky. He's one of the good ones."

"One of the good ones?"

"Not every vampire wants to be the way they are," she reminded. "There are a few vampires like him in here; they want to survive, but they don't like having to do it this way. They'd choose to be human again if they could."

This gave me a lot to think about. How many vampires felt like Silas? He wasn't the first I'd heard of to dislike being a vampire, but was that feeling more common than I thought? I didn't have time to ask more questions, though.

Kyoko escorted me to my room around seven in the evening, so I could get ready. After I showered, I did my makeup just as Kyoko told me to wear it, with bright red lipstick, light bronze eye shadow, and heavy mascara. I then slipped on a beautiful red formal gown I wasn't allowed to protest. I was instructed to wear my hair up in a high bun, so it didn't get in the way of Maurice drinking from my neck.

When I was done getting ready, I heard a knock at the door. Kyoko had come to bring me to the ballroom as she said she would at eight. It was seven forty-five, so she was early. But when I answered the door, it wasn't Kyoko. Colin was standing there with his fangs out, obviously thirsty for my blood.

This isn't good.

He grabbed me firmly and pushed me down onto the bed. I screamed, while kicking frantically at him. I looked at the nightstand for something I could use as a weapon, but all I could reach was the alarm clock. I grabbed the clock and slammed it across his head, but he barely flinched. This only pissed him off more and he slapped me across the face. It stung, but it didn't halt my defenses.

"Colin, stop! Maurice will kill you!" I screamed again, hoping someone would hear me.

"Relax, Akasha. I just want a taste of your blood. I just need a few drops." Colin licked his lips.

"Maurice would never allow that. He said my blood is forbidden, Colin. Please don't do this," I begged him, repeatedly. "Stop, Colin. Please don't!"

"I could smell your blood from outside the door. And why should my brother get to walk in the daylight while the rest of us suffer in eternal darkness?" He gripped my wrist tightly and he was surprisingly strong, given how skinny he looked. "He let Roland drink from you, but not his own brother," he said through clenched teeth.

I lifted my knee, ready to knee him in the groin, but Colin bit down on my neck. The pain was so excruciating, my body began to tremble. This time it wasn't as easy to relax, so my struggling made the pain even worse. I closed my eyes and thought about my friends, about Dorian and about Caleb. It was the only way to get through the experience. The pain started to subside and all I could feel was blood being drained from my body. Colin released me after a minute and climbed off my body, still sitting on the bed.

I was waiting for him to lick his lips like Roland did, but his reaction was unexpected. Colin stood there for a few minutes with a blank stare and blinked rapidly. He squinted his eyes and opened them as wide as he could. He quickly leaped off the bed and ran to the bathroom, pulled the lid up from the toilet and puked all the blood out he had stolen from me, spitting the last remaining blood from his mouth onto the floor. When he exited the bathroom, he just stood there and glowered at me. I climbed off the bed and stood in my fighting position, ready for him to strike. He was *not* going to touch me again.

"It's disgusting," he whined. Colin turned toward the door and ran out faster than he had entered. I relaxed my stance.

Disgusting?

Kyoko had said the taste of a witch's blood was like no other, and especially the blood from Spirit. I ran into the bathroom and looked at the two wounds on my neck that were almost healed. My eyes scanned the bathroom. There was blood everywhere.

I needed to clean this up or they'd know. There's no way I could tell Maurice what had happened. He would think I gave myself to Colin, and then he might punish me for it.

This would be my secret. I prayed he wouldn't notice Colin going out in the daylight before I escaped from this place.

He did throw it up, though. Is there enough of my blood in his system for the daylight powers to even work?

After cleaning up as much blood as I could from the sheets, I threw away the bloody towels and cleaned the toilet. I composed myself and waited on the bed for Kyoko. When she arrived, her eyes immediately targeted the bathroom. She sniffed the air.

"Akasha, what happened?"

Instantly, I realized I should have cleaned up better.

"I was touching up my makeup and dropped the powder compact and the mirror broke. I cut my fingers on the mirror edges as I was cleaning it up."

She looked at me suspiciously and mumbled something in Japanese while grabbing my hand. "Let's go. He is ready for you."

I entered the family room and all the witches, humans, and vampires were waiting for Maurice, who hadn't joined them yet. Sarah was the first to speak when Maurice entered the room.

"Everyone, on your knees," she instructed.

They all fell to one knee and bowed to him. I didn't move, but stared at him as he approached me.

"Mercy, you need to get down on your knees," Sarah whispered while keeping her head down.

He was now standing in front of me, with no expression on his face.

"I will not bow down to a vampire," I scowled. "I don't care what he can do to me."

Gasps came from the crowd.

Maurice chuckled and the vampires started to laugh uncomfortably around him, while the humans and witches looked frightened for me. Maurice lifted his hand as if to strike but I only stood there defiantly. I was done being afraid.

I will not give him the satisfaction of scaring me. Not anymore.

He didn't hit me like I thought he would. Instead, he turned my head to expose my neck. My heart began beating rapidly. I thought he would see the wounds from Colin, but he only stroked my neck softly. From his reaction, I could tell he saw no wounds.

"No reason in giving you any more punishment for speaking to me the way that you just did, when you are about to be fed upon," he said coldly with a huge grin on his face.

The crowded room was silent, waiting for his instructions. "Everyone, please join me in the ballroom," he commanded.

Maurice grabbed my hand softly and escorted me to the ballroom. Everyone followed behind. He leaned toward me as we were walking and with a firm tone said to me, "I will not be disrespected in front of my clan. Noah will be here shortly with your friend and you won't have much of a choice but to abide."

A part of me felt like it was just an empty threat. Abigail was watching her. She would never let something bad happened to her. If Abigail couldn't fight off whoever came for them, there was also Caleb, my family, and the werewolves. Could they really have gotten to Shannon?

"Screw you, you blood sucking demon. When I find a way to get this bracelet off my wrist, you will be the first to die at my hands." I instantly regretted this threat. The look on his face was pure rage.

"I am not afraid of a witch. Especially one with a very big ego," he barked backed and squeezed my wrist.

I am the one with the big ego?

I wanted to share those thoughts with him, but once I entered the ballroom, I only focused on the rows of vampires, that were ready to watch me get devoured. The only thing I thought about was, how the hell was I getting out of this?

CHAPTER TWENTY EIGHT

At the front of the room was a stage covered in black and red roses. Maurice walked me to the front of the stage and sat me down. It all looked a little too pretentious to me. Was he really going to dip me down over a bed covered in rose petals, like some cheesy romance novel?

I looked around the room that was surrounded by tall windows and smaller ones that could be opened slightly to let the breeze in from the outside. Now that it was the evening, several windows were opened and the curtains drawn. I took a deep breath in as a cool breeze entered the room. Oh, how I wanted to be outside instead of in that suffocating ballroom.

I eyed the rows of seats in front of the stage. Everyone was still taking their seats and each witch or human had to sit next to their vampire. This was going to be a blood bath the moment he took a bite out of me. This wasn't just a time for Maurice to feed on his witch for the first time, but a time they could all join in on a feeding together. Every witch or human with longer hair was wearing their hair up in a ponytail or bun.

Dorian was standing next to the stage with his hands clasped together, staring up at me. Ever since I had arrived, I'd noticed he didn't have a donor or a slave like everyone else. Once I made eye contact with him, he walked toward me and pulled the red scarf that had been wrapped around his neck. He proceeded to wrap the scarf around my bun.

"What's this for?" I asked him softly. Being this close to him again made butterflies flutter in my stomach. Oh how I wished I could just hold him again and kiss him tenderly like we did every evening we snuck away from our homes to meet each other. I weakened at the knees when I breathed in his intoxicating scent.

"It's just tradition." He tightened the scarf slowly around the bun and then stepped away from me.

"What are you doing, Dorian?"

I lowered my eyebrows at him. He frowned and turned away from me to face Maurice.

"Dorian, where is Colin?" Maurice asked.

"I haven't seen him. Do you want me to go find him?" he answered steadily.

"No, I have waited long enough." He smiled, sniffed my neck, and protruded his fangs. He then pushed me down to my knees. I glared up at him as a warning.

I'm going to fight you, Maurice. I am going to fight.

A dark-skinned man wearing a top hat and a sleek gray suit walked onto the stage. He recited his chant and gently wafted the smoke from sage around us. He circled us a few times till we were surrounded by a strong earthy, herbaceous scent. I assumed this was the witch Maurice was telling me about. The witch continued his chant.

I had to think of something and fast. Maurice was the last vampire in the world I wanted to have the kind of power my blood would give. Then suddenly, I felt something on my head.

The sensation was slipping from my hair where the scarf Dorian wrapped around my bun had been. As it was about to hit the floor, I caught it from behind me. I felt something hard on my palm. I tried to be secretive as I felt the hard object. Finally, I realized it was a key.

A key!

Dorian *was* on my side. I lowered my left hand and with my other hand, I unlocked the bracelet around my wrist using the key and I softly tucked the key and bracelet under my dress while keeping my wrist hidden.

Maurice held me firmly in his arms, lowering my body so my neck was exposed. He was already inches from my neck, but he joined in on the chant the witch was reciting. I closed my eyes and did what I had done with the water at the cove.

I focused on what I wanted my powers to do. There was no chanting, no herbs, and no spell book this time. My mind was the only thing in control as I mustered all the energy I could.

What am I capable of right now? How much power can I control at once?

My hand opened, with my palm facing up, as I focused my energy on all five elements. The elements were speaking to me. The bucket in the corner of the stage was only a few feet from us. Looking at it, I commanded it to move, using the energy force from my fingertips. My fingers tingled slightly, right as the bucket wobbled.

I closed my eyes tightly, but this time, I focused on the trees outside the walls of the house. I saw their branches reaching for the windows, and they hovered there, shaking and waiting for my command. Maurice was still chanting, and every vampire grabbed their slave and was ready to bite down.

I'd never tried to speak to nature before, but I knew I could do it. It was risky, but I had no other choice. Time was running out.

"Trees ... save me," I spoke out loud.

"What?" Maurice's attention was broken from the ritual.

All at once, I felt energy moving through my body again, but with a stronger force, and I tried my best to conceal it from Maurice. He looked down at me, his eyes wide, and he grabbed my hand quickly to observe I no longer had the bracelet on my wrist.

I yanked my wrist from him and braced both hands on the stage, while using both feet to kick him away from me as hard as I could. The force of my kick caused him to go flying across the stage.

Whoa, I'm not just stronger in power now, but I have the physical strength to fight.

Hisses and gasps were coming from the other vampires, while I looked down at my hands which had a bright green glow radiating from them. The room was now shaking, walls were cracking, and everyone was scurrying around the room like roaches.

Maurice made his way back to me. He grabbed my throat, but I wouldn't crumble under his strength. I stayed still like a statue as magic flowed through my fingertips. He wouldn't let go of me.

A second later, I lifted both of my hands above my head and threw my arms out to the side, allowing the green energy to leave my fingers. Suddenly, a crash from the windows lining the ballroom echoed in my ears. Tree branches broke through the windows and into the ballroom, shattering the glass and thrusting their branches through vampire's hearts as they tried to run in the opposite direction.

My eyes narrowed in on a female vampire running toward me at lightning speed. The roots from one of the trees blasted through the floorboards at the center of the room, stopping her in her tracks. She tried to run in the opposite direction, but the root grabbed her by the leg, twisting her body and soaring her up into the air. She screamed and hit the roots with her fists, but the roots only squeezed tighter and tighter around her body until she exploded into ash.

Maurice turned around to focus his attention briefly on what was happening behind him and I kneed him in the groin, causing him to scream and release me. One of the vampires quickly jumped toward the stage, trying to stop me, but I kicked him in midair and he plummeted to the ground. It was a gruesome scene straight out of a horror movie.

Maurice was right behind me. He grabbed my arms and bent them backwards, forcing me to fall face forward onto the stage and lose focus on what I was commanding the trees to do. Everything came to a standstill. I tried to get up, but there were already three other vampires holding me down. One of them put the bracelet back on my wrist.

I looked around the room trying to find Dorian but didn't see him anywhere.

I prayed I hadn't hurt him.

Several vampires were screaming in the distance from wounds that hadn't healed yet, and many were lying on the floor in a pile of dust, while others were staring at me on the stage with fuming rage. Several humans and witches were crying for their now deceased vampires. I didn't understand it. They should have been happy they were free of them. I looked up at Maurice who was ready to sink his teeth into my neck. His anger seemed to grow as he observed all the death and destruction I had caused. I scanned the crowd for Dorian again, and spotted him coming to his feet. He was covered in his own blood.

What have I done?

The bloodied scene didn't seem to concern Maurice anymore. Apparently, all he wanted was my blood. Maurice licked his fangs and moved toward me while the vampires were still holding me down. He stopped moving when a loud voice echoed through the room.

"Stop! Maurice, don't!" Colin called out while running toward the stage.

Maurice grunted. "What is it? Where have you been?"

"Don't drink her blood. It's a trick. It's all been a lie!" Colin told him.

"What are you talking about, brother?" He signaled the vampires to pull me back up to my feet.

What the hell is happening?

"I'm sorry, Maurice, but I was tempted today to drink her blood. I couldn't stop myself," Colin said as he backed away from him. The look in Maurice's eyes said he wanted to kill his own brother in that moment.

"Noah, seize him," Maurice commanded.

Noah ran quickly to Colin and grabbed both of his arms. Maurice approached Colin and slapped him firmly across the face. Maurice quickly backed up. The skin on Colin's face turned pink where he had been slapped.

"Colin?" Maurice cried.

"Yes, brother. I am human. Blood is pumping through my beating heart and I feel weak and powerless. I can feel my heart beating." Tears formed in Colin's eyes.

More gasps filled the room as vampires heard what he had said, and my eyes widened as I realized what his words meant.

CHAPTER TWENTY NINE

"That's it," I said out loud. "My blood allows a vampire to walk in the light, not because of some temporary power, but because it turns them back to a human. Roland knew it this entire time, too." I smiled. "This was the reason for my existence. The power of Spirit brings light."

I turned to Colin. "Your soul is your light. My blood reunites your body with your soul again." I laughed and turned to Maurice. "Did you really think it was going to be this easy?"

"How is this possible?" Maurice cried and flung his hand toward my throat.

Dorian leaped toward us, but Noah grabbed the back of his shirt and pulled him back before anyone else noticed.

Noah must know about us.

Maurice squeezed harder around my throat and threw me across the stage. I slammed hard against the wooden floor and winced.

"This is impossible!" he screamed.

Maurice slowly walked toward me as I lay on the floor in agony. "I did not wait centuries for you, just to be deceived." He tightly gripped the bun on my head and pulled me up.

He held me high in the air. "I love being a vampire. Nothing is better than the strength I hold and the power I have over you pathetic humans. I will not have you destroy what we have built here." He paused and composed himself. "How do you reverse it?"

I shook my head. "I don't know. I didn't know my blood would do this," I confessed.

Maurice released me, dropping me to the ground, and approached his brother with his fangs still out.

"Stop, Maurice," Kyoko said fearfully. "You don't know what will happen if you touch him. Don't risk it."

He paused for a brief moment and then turned back to Kyoko. "Kyoko, feed him your blood," he demanded.

"Master?"

"Do it!"

Kyoko bit her wrists and Colin gladly drank from it. They all watched Colin as Kyoko backed away.

While this was happening, I looked around the room and saw several vampires eyeballing me and licking their lips. I knew not every vampire in this room desired to be what they were. If they had a chance to be human again, they'd take it.

There was broken glass on the floor from the window and I stealthily picked it up without anyone seeing. I went to slice my hand, but Dorian was in front of me before the blade could touch my skin. He shook his head. "Don't, Mercy. Not yet."

I looked down at his bloodied shirt. "Dorian are you okay?

"I heal quickly, too, remember. The branches never pierced my heart."

"Dorian?" Maurice interrupted us. "Did you lose something?"

Maurice held up the key to my bracelet.

No, they can't take him from me. Not again.

I grabbed his arm and held on, but Noah and one other guard grabbed Dorian by the shoulder and pulled him away from me.

Noah looked down at Dorian. "Sorry my friend, I don't have a choice."

"Get him out of here," Maurice commanded. They escorted Dorian out of the ballroom and Maurice went over to Colin again, grabbed his neck, and snapped it. Colin fell lifeless to the ground.

I jumped, shocked at the sudden impulse to kill his brother. They all stared at Colin for a few minutes, waiting for him to wake, but he didn't move.

"Get up, Colin. Wake up!" But there wasn't any movement. Maurice screamed and kicked his brother. "Wake up!" He shouted again.

"You see, if you do that to a human, they die," I said to him with a slight smile.

Maurice screamed and moved toward me. He struck me across the face. Right at that moment, the lights in the ballroom went dark.

Someone came up behind me, covered my mouth, and pulled me behind the stage curtains. One arm was wrapped around my waist as another pulled around and placed a hand over my bracelet. I felt the sensation of burning around my wrist. I winced as the bracelet melted off and fell to the floor. The strong arm that wrapped tightly around my waist was familiar. It was Caleb.

I quickly turned around and threw my arms over his shoulders, holding him tight. "Caleb! Where is everyone?" There was panic in my voice and I tried to catch my breath.

"They're safe. We were able to hide Shannon before they got to her," Caleb explained as I released him.

Those words sent a wave of relief but there was still Cami. "And Cami? Has anyone checked on her at the hospital?"

"Joel sent Lily through a portal to the hospital so she could move her body. Don't worry. She's safe at your home, too." I let go of the air I had been holding in. My friends were safe.

"They told me they captured her."

"They lied. I'll explain everything on the way."

He grabbed my hands and led me off the stage.

"Wait! We have to save Dorian. They are going to kill him," I said. "I can't leave him."

"We cannot save him right now, Mercy. We can come back for—" He stopped. The look on his face showed me that he knew I was aware he had lied to me.

I frowned at him. "Yes, the same Dorian. You lied to me"

His face grew grim. "I was just protecting you from a world of hurt. He joined this clan on his own. I wanted you to have good memories of him."

"That's a lie!" I said sharply.

"Let's talk about this later. We have to go."

We heard Maurice shouting orders to his men and I knew Caleb was right. We needed to leave, but I would come back for Dorian. I would come back for everyone behind these walls that didn't want to be here.

It took us over ten minutes to find the back door that led out to the garden on the side of the property. It was so dark out that we couldn't see where we were walking anymore. Caleb held up his hand and a flame lit on each fingertip.

"What are you doing?" I asked.

"We need light."

I followed closely behind him.

The air around us was refreshing as it entered my lungs. I took several deep breaths. We were free. Well, almost.

"How did Shannon escape?" I asked. "They said they got into the safe house."

"Some of their men disconnected the power to the safe house and the door we had her locked behind was no longer secured.

Abigail was able to get her out on time through another passage way through the sewers and took her to your house," he explained. He opened up another door that led through the garden behind the property. "They were right behind them but Abigail is fast. She was able to make it on time to Joel's portal."

I sighed with relief, but my relief was short-lived as the flood lights turned on as we approached the property gates.

We turned our attention toward Maurice as he cleared his throat. Standing on each side of him were Noah and Kyoko.

"Going somewhere?" Maurice asked.

"It's over, Maurice. You can't stop us," I said.

Caleb pulled his hand out and a ball of flames circled the top of his palm. He didn't throw it. He just looked at Maurice with fuming rage.

"I know about the dagger. I'll find it." His threat didn't faze me one bit. This blood sucker wasn't going to win and he was no longer going to scare me.

"Then I'll be waiting," I threatened back.

Maurice turned around and moved to the side, letting us pass. I was puzzled as to why he would just let us go, until I saw Riley and Amber in their wolf forms, approaching the property. Caleb closed his hand, releasing the power of Fire.

Maurice and Kyoko looked terrified, still staring at Riley and Amber.

"Like I said, you can't stop us," I repeated as we crossed each other, slightly bumping my shoulder against his arm. "Goodbye, Maurice."

Caleb and I picked up our speed and ran toward the pack.

Caleb led me to an open portal about a mile from the house. We were then teleported to the front porch of my home. Once I saw the house, I stood there, relief finally hitting me. My heart felt heavy. We were safe, but Dorian was not.

CHAPTER THIRTY

"Leah, Ezra, and Simon are here. We are finally a coven again. They're excited to see you," Caleb said.

I wanted to be happy in this moment. My coven was my family and I hadn't seen them since I had died. They were a part of me and I a part of them. But I felt empty in that moment. I took one step forward and a bright light radiated on the front of the house, but it was coming from behind me. I turned around and the light was so bright I had to close my eyes.

The light slowly dimmed and a beautiful woman in a long, white dress stood in front of me.

I recognized the angel as she approached. Caleb stood between us. "Don't come any closer."

"I'm not going to hurt her," she said softly.

"No? I find that hard to believe after she killed your son."

"The world has one less monster. I came here to thank her." Tatyana looked over at me with a gentle smile.

"Thank you, Caleb, for trying to protect me. But I'm not afraid of her," I explained, hoping he would back down.

She walked around Caleb elegantly, and reached out her hand. I touched it and I felt warmth and power fill my body. I lowered my hand.

"Caleb, please leave us," I ordered, but his hands clenched.

"Not a chance." He shook his head and took a few steps closer to me, but I held my hands up.

"I'm not asking for your permission," I snapped.

Caleb glared at me for a hard moment and threw up his hands. He walked to the side of the porch and plopped down on the rocking chair by the front door. He looked upset, but he apparently knew this wasn't an argument he was going to win. After I saw he wasn't going to protest anymore, I followed Tatyana toward the driveway, so we had some privacy to speak.

Tatyana turned toward me and smiled.

"Thank you for killing him. I couldn't do it, but he had to die. He would destroy this world if he hurt you. You five are my greatest creation, especially you, Mercy."

It was such a weird thought, that we had been created by an angelic being, to kill the very thing she created in the first place. I knew though, that without her guidance, I couldn't do this.

"I need your help, Tatyana. I can't do this alone."

"Of course you can. All of you can." Her voice was so calm and gentle, but that's to be expected coming from an angel, I guess.

"Will you save Dorian from Maurice's clan? Please? Save as many as you can from that place. He was taken for saving me. That is, if they haven't already killed him."

"I will try to save Dorian and take down that house. I will rescue those who want saving behind those walls, but it's your mission to fight vampires, Mercy, not mine anymore. I failed once, and now it's your turn to restore the balance that was lost because of my mistake."

I turned to Caleb and then back to Tatyana. "How do I do this? How do I fight this fight?"

She smiled gently and walked closer to me. "You love them both, don't you?"

I nodded. "Caleb is complicated and frustrating, but my heart aches whenever he touches me. And Dorian ..." I paused and tears began to fill my eyes. "Dorian is the love of my life."

She lowered her head to my ear and whispered. My eyes widened, and I couldn't hold back the tears that stung my eyes.

I looked up at her again, nodding my head. "Thank you."

She bowed her head, extended her wings, and took off into the sky.

"Roland is almost here," Caleb said as he stepped down from the porch.

I wiped the tears on my face. "You can't trust him. He purposely led me out of the vampire lair at the cemetery so I'd get caught."

"I know."

"You knew?" I said furiously.

"I didn't know then, of course, but after he became human, he came back here to help us. He needed your blood to become a witch again. He's a powerful witch and he needed to be human again to use the kind of magic we need in this fight. Maurice wasn't going to let him leave if he didn't give you up."

"And Dorian ... was he all part of this plan, too?" He was silent.

"You knew he was alive, Caleb. You lied to me."

He walked up to me, hesitated, and placed his hand on my cheek. "Mercy, please don't."

I pushed his hand away from my cheek. "Stop, Caleb! You purposely kept me from him. Why?"

"Because I love you and I'm selfish. You and I had something special, and it was ripped apart by parents that didn't understand the kind of love we had for each other. You met Dorian the day we were forced to stop having a relationship. You gave your heart to him."

He stepped closer to me, causing me to have to take a step back so we weren't touching. "I also thought keeping that secret would protect you from being in the arms of someone I never trusted. We have a chance to start over again. Dorian and you could never have what we had." He put his hand under my chin and lifting it gently. "He's a vampire, Mercy; he's the very thing you were sent here to kill."

I shook my head. "That isn't your decision to make, Caleb." I grabbed his hand and removed it from my chin. "Your father and Abigail are vampires and you still love them."

"They're my family."

"And Dorian was mine."

He backed up slightly. "I'll fight for you."

I filled in the gap between us and lightly touched his hand. "I do love you, Caleb. But I also love Dorian."

I lowered my head but kept my hand gently in his, afraid of the words that I had to say next. They were words that he had to hear, and something I had to do to fulfill our given mission.

"Tatyana is going to rescue Dorian from that clan and anyone who wants to leave, but the fight isn't going to stop there. There are more to clans to destroy and humans and witches to save." I choked back the sobs that were threatening to escape.

Caleb stood there in silence, tears now filling his eyes.

I let go of his hand. "I can't let my feelings for you and Dorian distract me from what we were sent here to do. Your father was right. We were never sent here to fall in love."

"Please don't, Mercy." He reached for me but I held up my hands.

I closed my eyes as a ray of white light poured from my fingertips. I opened my eyes and formed a bright white ball with the light. The ball grew larger and brighter, my hands swarming around it, keeping it strong and bright. I whispered to myself the words Tatyana had spoken in my ear. I pulled the ball in toward my chest, almost falling over by the force of energy entering my body.

"What are you doing?" he yelled, taking a step toward me.

I looked up at this man that I had once loved. All the feelings I'd had for him in the past and in my current life were gone. I thought about Dorian and everything we used to have and the feelings I had when I had seen him again. Nothing was there. They were two beautiful men I knew cared for me, but the only feelings I had in my heart were memories.

"Mercy, what did you do?" he asked, panic echoing in his voice.

"The angel showed me how to take it away, Caleb. I had to take it all away."

He moved back slightly and fell to the floor on his knees. He realized what I had done.

"I'm sorry, Caleb. But the only feeling I have now is the desire to kill every one of those blood sucking demons and purify our world once again."

The Dark Awakening is book one in The Chosen Coven Series.

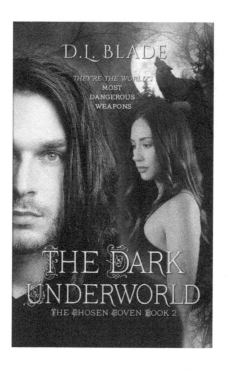

To be Directed to book two, click the title:

The Dark Underworld

ACKNOWLEDGMENTS

Thank you to all my beta readers, and my editor who acted as a mentor on several occasions.

I also want to give a special thank you to my husband, who supported me when I gave up my career in real estate to fulfill a dream I have: to be a published author. He has been such an incredible support, and I couldn't do this without him.

ABOUT THE AUTHOR

Diana Lundblade grew up in California and studied at the California Healing Arts College, going on to work as a massage therapist for thirteen years. Diana now lives in Colorado, where she worked as a real estate agent for a time, before deciding to concentrate on her family and writing.

Diana always loved writing, concentrating on poetry rather than prose when she was younger. That changed, however, when she had a dream one night and decided to write a book about it.

In her spare time, Diana enjoys a wide variety of hobbies, including reading, writing, attending rock concerts, and spending time outdoors with her family, camping and going on outings.

In the future, Diana hopes that she can continue to write exciting novels that will captivate her readers and bring them into the worlds that she creates using her imagination.

CPSIA information can be obtained
at www.ICGtesting.com
Printed in the USA
FSHW010506040919
61696FS

9 780578 416458